MEET ME HERE

BRYAN BLISS

GREENWILLOW BOOKS
An Imprint of HarperCollins*Publishers*

Meet Me Here

Copyright © 2016 by Bryan Bliss

All rights reserved. No part of this book may be used or reproduced in any manner whatsoever without written permission except in the case of brief quotations embodied in critical articles and reviews. Printed in the United States of America. For information address HarperCollins Children's Books, a division of HarperCollins Publishers, 195 Broadway, New York, NY 10007.

www.epicreads.com

The text of this book is set in 11-point Sabon MT.

Book design by Paul Zakris

Library of Congress Cataloging-in-Publication Data is available.

ISBN 978-0-06-227538-7 (trade ed.)

16 17 18 19 20 CG/RRDH 10 9 8 7 6 5 4 3 2 1

First Edition

 GREENWILLOW BOOKS

FOR NORTH CAROLINA,
WHICH IS IN MY BONES

CHAPTER ONE

This is supposed to be the best night of my life. That's what all the cards say, what every person at this party believes as they yell and raise their hands in the air, high-fiving while some cover band tunes their instruments in the corner of the living room. And when people come up to say hello—to wax nostalgic—of course I smile. I clink the beer I'm not going to drink against their red cups, nodding intently as they wish me the best—when they ask me about my brother.

These are the final hours. And nothing—not graduation, or Jake, or even a natural disaster—can stop me from getting in my truck and disappearing once the sun comes up.

No answers, no hesitation—just *gone*.

Another well-wisher is strolling toward me when the entire room gasps, one collective mouth yelling, "Daaaammmmmn!" I turn with everyone else, just catching Mallory Carlson's hand coming back and her boyfriend holding his nose, looking like he's going to cry.

The entire party stops moving. We're all waiting to see if he'll really start bawling or maybe if she'll drop him with another right. His lip is wavering and her fist is still cocked and everybody—every single person at this party—is certain of one thing: Mallory's going to put him down. Instead, she looks around the room, skimming from face to face until she finds mine.

Mallory doesn't hesitate. Walks right up to me, hands still fists, looking ready to punch me, too.

"Do you have your truck?"

I stare at her.

She thumps me on the chest once, ignoring the yells and the laughter, focusing on me and speaking slow. Like I'm stupid and she didn't just try to KO her boyfriend.

"Your *truck*, Thomas. I need you to drive me home."

This girl's a ghost, a legend I used to believe in; if I were to reach out and touch her, there wouldn't be anything there.

She sighs.

I was six and she wanted my swing; that's how it started. When I went home, my dad almost looked proud that I'd gotten into a fight. He held my face in his hands, studying the only black eye I've ever had. I didn't tell him it was a girl, and we spent the night in the driveway, practicing how to throw and, in my case, dodge a punch. That next day I tried to avoid her, but Mallory came marching up to me on the playground. I had my hands up, protecting my face like Dad showed me. All she did was shake her head.

People laugh. Somebody yells, "Watch out, Bennett, you're next!" I expect her to whip around, offering both middle fingers to the party—to steer an already grand graduation story into legendary territory. Maybe drop a few more bodies in the process, anyone unlucky enough to be close.

She closes her eyes and says, "Please, Thomas."

That's it. No explanation for why she just hit Will or why she can't get any of her other friends to take her home. Why she decided to talk to me tonight for the first time in seven years. Just "Please."

I used to live for every half-cocked idea that came off her lips. When we were kids, it was me and her and nothing else. My dad always said it wasn't right for a boy to be playing with a girl that much, and what were we even doing anyway? It didn't help that I could never account for those hours. How the day would end and we never saw it coming, running home as fast as we could, cackling like mad.

But how many chances like this have we explicitly avoided? How many times has she walked by me in the hallways, suddenly becoming really interested in the lockers or a phantom stain on her jeans? And fine, people move on. Things change. It still doesn't explain why she's here in front of me now.

Before I can say a word, she holds up a hand and says, "Whatever. I'm sorry I asked."

And then she's gone.

It takes one second for me to feel like an asshole. Two more before my feet move, trying to catch Mallory as she slips through the crowd.

The catcalls start—"Get it! Yeah, boy!"—and I want to stop the music, the chatter, get the attention of the entire party and explain how inseparable she and I used to be, how there was a time before high school, before middle school, when the idea that we wouldn't talk for a day—let alone seven years—would be inconceivable.

How do you describe a constant companion? A person who knows everything about you, no matter how big or small? As she disappears out the door, I wish I still believed that fundamental parts of your life couldn't change in a moment.

When I finally get outside, she's halfway across the yard, cussing loudly and pulling off her shoes. I jog to catch up, calling her name. When she sees me, I expect her to tell me to get lost. Call me an asshole or worse. She reaches down, barely stopping to rub her heel.

"These shoes suck," she says, hopping once before starting back down the driveway.

Sounds of the party fill the night, bouncing off trees and car windows as I follow her toward the dark road. Mallory tiptoes around a broken bottle, detouring into the grass. I tiptoe around our history, everything else.

"I wasn't trying to be a prick," I say. "You surprised me."

"Well, isn't that the story of the night? Everybody's surprised. Listen, all I need is a ride home. If you can do that for me, great. If you can't, then fine. I'll walk."

She bends over to rub her heel again, cussing even

louder. When she stands up, she faces me. "Thomas, I'm sorry. I just—I can give you gas money if you want."

"It's like five miles. I don't need gas money."

What else can I say? I've seen her at school, of course. We were even assigned a group project during junior year. But Wayne was in the group, and he's loud enough that I could sit there, not saying a word, listening and laughing as he flirted and carried on with every girl in the group, Mallory included. When we finally gave the presentation and I was back sitting in my seat, I swear it was the first time I took a breath in two weeks. Things went back to normal, both of us pretending the other didn't exist.

Behind us, a voice calls Mallory's name. Will is still wearing his graduation hat, the shirt and tie. All of it askew. One of his buddies follows him, stumbling down the driveway, a laughing shadow. Mallory starts walking. "Go back to the party, Will."

He brushes past me and tries to grab Mallory's hand. "Talk to me."

"I did; you didn't listen."

"All I want is for you to explain it to me. Please."

He sounds desperate, almost scared. The way my mom sounded a year ago, when she learned Jake's unit had been attacked. Like there was nothing she could do, least of all understand what the army officer was telling her about her son. Injured in action. A hospital in Germany. Lucky to be alive.

The first day I saw Jake after he was wounded, he didn't look much different. Skinnier maybe. He'd been shot in the shoulder, but there were no missing limbs, no visible scars. When he walked into our house—the way he had thousands of times before—I was so damn happy. But he was messed up worse than any of us could have ever imagined. We just didn't see it yet.

"Let's go," Mallory says.

At first I don't realize she's talking to me, that we can see my truck now, the same one she rode in as a kid. My dad was still driving it then. We'd hop in the back any chance we got, even if it meant suffering through a trip to the hardware store and my dad's constant looks in the rearview mirror.

She grabs my arm and pulls me across the road, Will following.

"Why are you doing this?" he asks.

"Maybe you should talk to him," I say, but Mallory ignores both of us, only letting go of my arm when we're next to the truck. She climbs up into the passenger seat, ignoring Will, who starts beating on the window and calling Mallory's name. When I walk around to the driver's side, Will meets me at the door. There's a shadow of a bruise on his face, but it's the way he scrambles toward me that really makes him look broken.

All he says is "Thomas, c'mon. I'll talk to Mallory. You can go back to the party."

That's the smartest option. Get Mallory out of my truck and go back to the party, back to pretending that this is the best night of my life and in fact my brother— my entire future—hasn't gone up in flames. But how long does that last? An hour? Maybe two? I still have to go home, still have to see Jake sitting there cold and empty. I still have to face tomorrow morning, when I finally don't show up at the recruiter's office. The moment everybody I've ever known will mark me as a liar and a coward.

I'm tired of pretending tomorrow isn't a reckoning. That I'm not scared to death about what I have to do. Every last ounce of *pretending* inside me is gone.

Will couldn't know this, of course. Couldn't know that maybe the only thing he could say that would make me get in the middle of a lovers' quarrel tonight is "You can go back to the party."

"Sorry, man."

I push past him and jump in the truck. He starts banging on my window, telling me he's going to do all sorts of things to me—that I'll regret this. Threats without teeth, because as soon as I turn the ignition, his voice pitches up an octave.

"Are you kidding me?"

Will walks with us as I put the truck in gear and slowly pull onto the road. He even runs beside us for a few steps before I get out of first gear. But soon we're moving too fast and he can't keep up.

And then it's just me and Mallory once again.

CHAPTER TWO

These roads are in my blood, and that's how I drive them: fast, with the windows rolled down. Letting the early-summer air crash into the cab as we pick up speed. I know every turn, every pebble.

And seeing Mallory in the passenger seat, biting the side of her thumb, kicks something alive in my stomach, a strange expectation. It's hearing your favorite song come on the radio or that first day of summer vacation. This is what our friendship could've become. Riding around with the windows down and the radio turned up. I shake my head, trying to focus.

"I shouldn't have hit him," she finally says. "That was a mistake."

"He looked pretty upset," I say.

She turns to face me, worried. "Like how upset? If you had to rate him from one to ten, what would he be? A five maybe?"

"Five sounds about right," I say, turning back to the road. But Will was an easy ten, and maybe higher. Whatever she said had him freaked. She nods once, twice.

"Yeah, he'll be fine," she says. "He'll be fine."

We're next to my grandpa's field, minutes from both our houses, when the headlights first appear behind us, just pinpricks. The car is riding my ass in seconds, then whipping into the left lane. Another dude living out his NASCAR fantasy, I think, slowing down to let him pass. But it's Will hanging out the window, gesturing wildly and yelling into the wind.

I glance at Mallory. "Do you want me to stop?"

She shakes her head, and I hit the gas; but his friend Jeremy's new Mustang keeps pace with us easily. Will keeps rising up out of the window, eyeing the truck's bed like he's thinking of taking a chance, so I slow down, make the angle more problematic. Every time Will yells for her, Mallory shrinks farther down in the seat.

An oncoming car forces Will and his friend to slingshot

behind us. They give me the high beams, ride my bumper. And then he's right back next to us, tossing out insults at me, my truck. Begging Mallory to hear him.

Jeremy fires his engine and races in front of me, hitting the brakes as soon as they clear my front end. I cut the wheel as I stop but still nearly put us in the ditch. Will jumps out, holding out his hands like he's trying to feel his way through the night. I've got my seat belt off and the door half open when Mallory grabs my forearm and says, "Please don't."

"Mallory, get out of the truck," Will says. "You can't say something like that and then disappear."

I expect Mallory to lean out the window and tell him exactly what he can do with himself, but she's down so low on the seat that I'm not sure she can even see above the dash.

"What do you want me to do?" I ask. "Run them over?"

I'm half smiling at the thought of going monster truck on Jeremy's car. I try to imagine their faces; the stories people would tell when they saw the twin black streaks of rubber across his hood tomorrow morning. What else could you expect from a night with Mallory? But whatever fueled her boxing display has disappeared. She refuses to look at Will or me, shaking her head rapidly back and forth. Smaller by the second.

Will's only a few feet away from us when she says, "Go. Please. I can't do this."

Her voice is tiny, frantic, and she's not looking at me when I nod. When I cut the wheel to the right and climb the small embankment, steering into the dark field. Mallory grabs the Oh Shit! handle above her window as we hit a rut, the entire cab jumping, and roar into the tall grass.

A few seconds later headlights pour into the darkness behind us.

"Jesus, they're really going to follow us. Out here. In that car?" I turn to Mallory. "Your boyfriend's a real dumbass, you know that, right?" She doesn't object or say anything, but when I turn my attention back to the field, I swear she nods.

The Mustang takes the embankment faster than I did, flying into the field. They're whooping out the windows as Jeremy cuts the wheel left and then right, fishtailing toward us.

As soon as they'd pulled that shit on the road, nearly wrecking the truck, Jake would've been out and in their face, restoring honor to the Bennett name with a few simple but pointed words. Embodying everything I've never been able to muster—the duty, the courage—in all my eighteen years. There'd be two choices for Will: get your ass going or get your ass beat.

But what Jake *would've* done is past tense. The time before he became a blank wall. And that says nothing of Mallory, who is pale as the moon. I cut the wheel hard to the right, hoping I can outrun Will and Jeremy to one of the back roads. As I do, the tires raise a clump of mud high in the air. It lands on the windshield with a thud, and Mallory jumps.

Mud.

I hit the wipers, and as they work back-and-forth—*Mud*.

"Hold on," I say.

I push the truck forward even faster, away from the road and toward the woods, black and toothy in the near distance. Mallory has been here how many times? Has run through this field in her bare feet, getting stuck up to her knees in the mud that's present no matter what season it is. Does she know where I'm headed now? Does she remember, too?

Either way, I hit the gas.

It's time to end this.

If you live in North Carolina and own a truck, you know about mud. It's you and your buddies hopping into the cab with a mind for the sort of aimless joy that is being covered head to toe, bumper to bumper. And this particular field, owned by my grandpa and soon to be passed down to my dad, is an abyss for any vehicle not jacked up a good ten inches.

They're never going to get that Mustang out.

When we hit the mud, it's like Moses parting the sea: a shower on both sides of the truck. Or maybe it's a baptism because as soon as that mud goes flying, Mallory finally comes to life, unleashing a banshee-wildcat howl that nearly pulls my hands from the steering wheel. Mud spits in the window, a thick stripe of it now on her cheek, her dress. She keeps screaming as I push the accelerator, kicking the wet earth up to the sky.

Will and Jeremy don't know what's happening until it's too late. The ground swallows the front wheels of their car, locking them in place. When it happens, I almost feel bad. The road's a half mile back, and they'll look like escaped convicts by the time they make it out. But that doesn't stop me from circling back one time and covering the Mustang.

When we're a hundred yards away, I cut my lights,

letting the high moon show me the way across the field, toward the gravel road at the end of the property. I slow down until I can hear my tires rolling over the grass. We're almost to the road when a train track glints in the darkness, sparking a memory so true, so deep I nearly slam on the brakes.

The bridge is nothing but concrete and rebar, no different from countless others in this town, but as soon as we pull up on it, I smile. I kill the engine and stare at the overgrown weeds, the dead leaves piled in one corner. The only sound is crickets as Mallory wipes mud from her face and picks a couple of stray clumps from her hair. We could be kids again, still angry that summer was over.

Mallory brushes another clump from her arm. "Do you remember when your brother came down here and we threw rocks at him?"

I nod. There hasn't been a worse beating in my life, first from my dad and then from my brother the next day. "God. What were we thinking?"

"He wanted to build a skateboard ramp down here— him and his friend. What was his name?"

"Tony," I say.

They haven't talked since Jake went off to basic training and Tony became a bagger at SuperMart. The few times I saw him, he never asked about Jake—still doesn't. Every friend Jake ever had acts like he's a ghost.

"I heard Jake came home at Christmas." She looks at her lap as she says it, and I know what comes next: "How's he doing?"

It's a question I've answered a thousand times since he came back. "Good," I always say. "Never been better," I tell them. Not because it's true; because it's easier. Nobody wants their war heroes broken. They want simple answers, ones that don't involve an emptiness so present in Jake that it's like he never existed any other way. They don't want to know how much he's changed, only to wish him the best, God bless America.

But even if I were going to be honest, how would I answer Mallory? How can I possibly explain what's wrong with Jake now? He isn't the guy who chased us out from under this bridge, yelling as we ran laughing into the summer sun. He isn't anything lately.

"Yeah. At Christmas." I hesitate. "He's okay."

"Will you tell him I said hello?"

"Yep."

And then the crickets again. A firecracker—or maybe a gunshot—somewhere in the distance. And Jake, of course, hanging over everything like a cloud.

When he came home, they paraded him up and down the streets of our small town like a beauty queen, riding in the back of a shockingly red convertible on loan from Hickory Chevrolet. All I'd ever wanted to be was like him, and no more so than in those first days he was back. It didn't take long to figure out there was something wrong. I could see it in his face, so tight and forced. The way he'd get whenever Kelly Simpson would come by the house his freshman year. Like he couldn't get away fast enough.

"Thomas." Mallory turns around in the seat, both knees tucked underneath her. There's a spot of mud on her nose, her chin. "Do you ever think about, you know, us? Back then?"

"Sometimes. Sure."

The truth is, it comes in waves, like a jet crossing over my house at night. But just like a passing plane, those deafening seconds, when I forget what it's like to hear, it ultimately passes. And then I don't think about Mallory Carlson for months, longer.

"We had some good times," Mallory says, her voice turning as generic as a yearbook inscription. One step removed from her punching me in the shoulder and making me promise we'll "Keep in touch" because "We finally graduated," double exclamation point.

Mallory stretches her legs out and yawns. "We should probably get going. I don't want them to try and find us."

I don't start the truck, don't reach for the keys. How many times did I hope for a nearly identical situation? For her to come back and demand an apology? Even in my daydreams I didn't have the courage to walk up to her and finally say: "I am sorry." And now that the opportunity has finally presented itself, as Mallory lazily picks dried pieces of mud from her arm, I can't escape the feeling that maybe I'm the only one who's been carrying this around for the past seven years.

The heat starts in the back of my neck, and soon my entire body is flush with embarrassment.

"All right, then. Let's get you home."

I swallow anything else I could say to her. Apologies, jokes: I zip everything up inside and present her the same face I give everyone. Happy, confident Thomas.

I start the truck and slowly back away from the bridge.
She doesn't move, doesn't say a word as we drive to her
house—still painted white, still chipped and worn—and
she opens the door of my truck and runs up her driveway
without looking back.

CHAPTER THREE

When I pull into our driveway, Mom and Dad are framed in the window, sitting at the table with Jake. It looks so normal, like Sunday dinner. Mom smiling and upbeat. Dad acting as if nothing's wrong. And Jake, void as usual. I almost throw the truck into reverse and pull away right then, leaving everything behind. And if I had the money stashed in my duffel bag with me, maybe I would. Instead, I get out and take a few deep breaths before I walk inside the house.

"Hey, honey," Mom calls.

Dad looks up at me tired, as I enter the kitchen. "I'm surprised you're back so early."

I don't look either of them in the eyes as I grab an apple and take a bite.

"Typical graduation party."

Mom smiles and Jake stares, his eyes distant and pitted like a Halloween mask. When he shifts, I notice the backpack at his feet—black and always present. I let my eyes linger on it for a moment, trying to guess what's inside, why he keeps it with him, no matter if he's going to the store with Mom or to the other room. Did he have it when he first came back? Probably, but I didn't notice.

"I said good-bye to some people," I say, forcing myself to look away from the backpack and into my mom's eyes. "Had a slice of pizza. Listened to some music. Talked to Mallory."

I know I've messed up as soon as I say it. Dad doesn't react, but Mom perks up.

"Mallory?" Mom asks. "Mallory Carlson?"

For the past few weeks my conversations with Mom have been nothing more than cursory. A simple report of the night, delivering the information I know she wants to hear. I take another bite of the apple.

"Yeah, that Mallory. I gave her a ride home, actually."

Mom always liked Mallory, and well into freshman year she would still sometimes drop little hints—"Why don't you give Mallory a call?"—as if it were as simple as just picking up the phone. As if the separation hadn't been anything other than intentional. Still, in her mind, it was the normal drifting apart that happens as you get older. Something that could be fixed. Would she believe how Dad told me it was time to grow up? That boys didn't play with dolls or wear pink, so why in the hell would I spend so much time with a girl?

Maybe. But it doesn't matter because I never picked up the phone.

"Fight with her boyfriend," I say. More apple. A casual shrug, because what's the big deal? Just another night, chomp-chomp. Shrug, shrug. Normal.

"You didn't get involved, I hope," Mom says, and I shake my head. "Well, good. Do you want dinner? You need more than an apple."

"Stop babying him," Dad says, eyeing me. "He should know if he needs to eat or not."

Nobody says anything until Mom forces a smile.

"It seems just like yesterday that this guy was graduating." Mom reaches over and tousles Jake's hair. He doesn't move, doesn't meet her eyes when she says: "Remember how much fun we had, Jake?"

I sat at this same table, not knowing what to say—trying to decide if I was excited or terrified. So I kept quiet and watched as my mom cried and Dad told her to stop. When Jake went to bed, he slapped me on the shoulder and told me not to do anything stupid while he was away. That he'd still be able to kick my ass, even from Afghanistan or wherever he'd end up. The next morning he was gone.

I wait for Dad to talk about how proud he was of Jake that morning, how proud he is still. But nobody speaks. Instead, he fiddles with the old kitchen clock. I can hear it ticking as I say, "Okay, I'm going to go finish getting ready."

"Already? I thought we could sit here and talk for a little longer," Mom says. Dad turns momentarily, looking me in the eyes before going back to the clock.

"I can't believe you haven't finished packing yet," he says.

"Only a few more things," I say.

He nods once, more a receipt on what he's just heard than an affirmation. He pops the back off the clock and picks up the tiny screwdriver sitting on the table. I don't think he's going to say anything else until he sighs and says, "One of these days you're going to figure out your priorities."

"Oh, stop it," Mom says, swatting him with a dish towel playfully. "It's his graduation."

He doesn't look up, doesn't say anything else. And he doesn't need to; just mark another one in the disappointment column. I give Mom a quick hug, and she holds my hand as I'm trying to walk away. I pause, letting her tether me to the kitchen for an extra second.

"Are you sure you're not hungry?"

I shake my head, trying to blind myself to everything happening—not happening—in the kitchen. We are the royal family of leaving things unsaid, of sweeping everything underneath the rug. And while I want to lay the blame solely on Mom and Dad, I know I'm just as guilty. I'm the one who's pretending to pack for a future that I gave up on months ago. I'm the one who's leaving because I don't have the courage to live up to my obligation. I don't stand for shit, and I know it.

Jake catches my eye, watching me with an inscrutable, catlike stare. It's a flash of clarity, quickly followed by the fade-out thing, where he's still staring but his mind is gone, flying into a completely different airspace.

Dad sighs. Shakes his head at the clock, me.

"I'm not hungry, Mom. Love you."

She squeezes my hand, and I hold on to it for another second, staring at Jake, willing her to look in his direction. To see what I see.

"Okay. Be careful."

She used to say, "I love you," when we left a room. But ever since Jake returned home, it's always fear for our safety. I walk out of the kitchen. Before I get to my room, Mom offers to bake chocolate chip cookies to the thick silence behind me.

I sit on my bed, pulling my duffel bag off the floor and onto my lap. Even if you searched it to the bottom, you wouldn't know that I wasn't shipping out in the morning. Pants, shirts, underwear—nothing unusual. I stare at the bag for the hundredth time, trying to find a mistake, a clue that when they come into my room tomorrow, I won't be here. That I'm throwing this bag in the back of my truck and driving as far as the $1,312 in my savings account will take me.

This was lawn-mowing money. "Give me a hand, and I'll throw twenty bucks your way" money. Saved through high school because that's what Bennetts were: disciplined. When my friends went to Myrtle Beach for spring break, I stayed home. When they bought hunting rifles and new rims for their trucks, I kept my debit card in my wallet. And now it was paying off, just not in a way I ever expected.

Sometimes when the entire house is quiet, when all I can hear is the wind outside my window, I try to imagine what would happen when tomorrow came. I had visions of me driving across the state line, music blaring. Of ending up in Montana, Wyoming, or even Oregon. It wasn't a plan as much as it was a way to escape, a detail that would come on me violently, pushing the air out of my lungs and doubt into my head.

What are you going to do when the money runs out?

How are you ever going to explain this?

You are making the biggest mistake of your life.

When I first committed, I was excited. Dad took me down to the recruiter's office to sign the papers, and I would've taken my uniform and gone right then if it hadn't been for high school and the hell Mom would've raised if I didn't graduate. I would finally be like Dad and Jake, a part of the brotherhood.

But that's gone. Because this isn't about signing a form and not showing up. It's shirking every piece of responsibility I've ever known in my life, and it makes me sick.

Everyone in this town thinks I'm cut from the same cloth as Jake, the fabric that makes a Bennett stand up and say: "I'm going to fight for your freedom." If you'd asked me before, I would've told you that dying was the worst thing that could happen to you. But now I know sometimes it's worse to come back alive.

There's a knock on my door, and I throw the duffel bag on the floor instinctively. As if whoever's waiting out there would be able to smell the deceit.

"Come in," I say, standing up because I know it's my dad. I get ready for the fight, the pep talk. They all sound the same lately. But when the door opens, it's Jake. He stands in the doorway staring at me, as if he needed a second invitation to cross the threshold.

"You ready for tomorrow?" he asks, readjusting the backpack on his shoulder before moving quickly and deliberately toward my bed. The suddenness of it shocks me. It's like a tiny drill sergeant somewhere inside him shouted, "Go!" and he responded. I freeze when he grabs my duffel bag and starts rummaging through it.

"You won't need half this shit," he says, sitting down. "They'll issue you everything."

There was a time I wouldn't dare bullshit Jake. He saw

every move I was going to make two seconds before I even had the idea.

"Yeah. You're probably right."

"And when you get there, it's going to be in your face. That's how they do it, okay? They're going to get on you right from the beginning, no matter what you do. There is no right or wrong that first day. Just shit, all around."

"Thanks."

Jake looks down at the duffel and then sets it back on the floor, his hands on his knees. He sits there like that for nearly a minute, grimacing at the carpet, before he pushes himself up and stands above me, searching for words.

"Anyway. I wanted to come in here. You know. Say good-bye. Good luck. That's it."

I assume we're going to hug or shake hands, and I get ready. I haven't touched him since the first day he came home, a shallow and awkward embrace. But he doesn't come any closer, just kind of shrugs and then walks slowly out of my room. Before he closes the door, he turns around and opens his mouth like there's more to say.

I wait, watching as the thought slips away. He nods once and closes my door.

A tiny pop, like a rock on a piece of tin, rings out. At

first I think it's my doorknob, that Jake's locked me in my room. But then it comes again, from my window. Birds sometimes fly into the glass from the tree in our backyard, but that's more of a sickening thud. The first time it happened, I couldn't look. Couldn't handle the way the bird twitched, unable to move but not ready to die. Dad took it around the corner, looking over his shoulder at me as he and Jake went to put the thing out of its misery. I couldn't sleep in my room for weeks afterward, sneaking into the den and praying I'd never hear a sound like that again.

But this isn't a bird. It comes once more, and then a fourth time. When I open my blinds, I nearly kill myself jumping backward.

Mallory waves hesitantly.

"What are you doing here?" I say.

She cups her hand to her ear theatrically, pantomiming an epic bout of confusion. Of hearing loss. When I don't open the window, she starts tapping on the glass even louder. And she doesn't stop—tap-tap-tap-tap—until I give in. As soon as she hears the lock click, she lifts the window as high as it goes.

"You're like a little kid," I say. But I might as well be talking to myself. She's got a hand on the sill and a foot against the metal siding, struggling to pull herself up.

"A little help here?"

I give her my hand, watching her kick up and eventually through my window the way she has a hundred times before. Once inside, she looks around for a moment. She's changed into jean shorts and a plain white T-shirt, more stylish than the ones she wore as a kid, but it's another forgotten memory. Did I ever see her in anything other than those ragged cutoffs?

"I like what you've done with the place." She points to a poster of a model in a bathing suit leaning against a jacked-up truck. "Don't let anyone tell you that isn't classy."

As soon as she says it, she looks away. As if she's embarrassed, too. We both stare at the carpet. I reach for my duffel, hoping it will end the conversation. A natural segue back to both of our regular lives. She grabs my hand like I'm about to touch fire.

"We should do something. Like right now—" She pauses as if her words required clarification. As if she were trying to preempt my coming objection. "I went home, and all I could think about is us under the bridge. That was fun, right? Basically, it's our graduation night, and we need to do *something*."

"I need to get up really early in the morning," I say.

But even the truth feels like a lie. And maybe it's because what I really want to say is much simpler: we barely know each other anymore. The fact that we even spoke to each other—let alone went to the bridge—is a gift. A chance to tie a bow on something I've admittedly regretted. But whatever magic we had as kids is gone, and there's nothing left to do or say. It's time to cut bait and thank the gods for getting a chance to remember how great we used to be, if only for an hour.

My door opens, and before I can turn around, Mallory goes rigid. Dad is normally unflappable, but when he sees me standing there with Mallory, his eyes go wide and his mouth drops open. Mom hovers behind him, and she's equally shocked but is able to get her mouth to work.

"Why, Mallory! What—how are you?"

As she hugs Mallory, I meet Dad's stare. His initial shock is gone, replaced by the same face I've seen all my life: eyes focused and unwavering, jaw set. Words do not follow this face because the message is clear: "You have made another poor decision. You should know better."

And I do. I want to tell him: "I don't want her here!" Because Mallory puts everything in jeopardy. This is the sort of attention I've tried to avoid for months. But as he keeps staring, as he refuses to speak, to even see that I'm trying to do my best with this, something breaks inside me.

Maybe it's the way he hasn't blinked or how he always assumes everybody's going to toe the line. To follow his orders. The injustice of it rises inside me, acid in my mouth. Why *shouldn't* I be able to go out with my friends—or whatever Mallory is at this point? Why does that matter at all? What is it hurting if I spend an hour not being a Bennett, not being some kind of perfectly stoic . . . soldier?

And I can't lie: I want to see his face when I go against him. I want to see the shock, the anger—all of it—when I tell him I'm leaving with her. To get even the smallest whiff of what it would be like to tell him my real plans.

"We're going out," I say. "Just for an hour."

Dad shakes his head, as if I were headed to the moon. "*Out?*"

Mallory nearly jumps with excitement. "We won't be gone long," she says.

"I'm sorry," Dad says. "Thomas is done for the night. I can drive you back to your house, if you need me to, but he isn't going anywhere."

"It's my graduation," I say. "And I'm ready."

"If you were ready, we wouldn't be having this conversation," he says to me. And then to Mallory: "I'll meet you in the driveway." He's already turned to leave my room when Mom speaks up.

"I don't think an hour is going to kill anyone."

Dad stops but doesn't face any of us. Mom never challenges him, rarely calls him out on the way he parents—like an iron fist. Sure, she'll come in behind him, patting me on the shoulder and telling me it's just how he is. That he loves us. But she never does this.

Dad still hasn't turned around when he finally says, "I expect you'll do what's right," and walks out of my room.

I look at Mom. She shakes her head and whispers: "Go have fun. But be back soon. Eleven, okay?"

I lead Mallory out of my room, not planning to stop until we're in my truck. Jake is still at the kitchen table, and Mallory pauses like she expects me to have a conversation with him, too. Or maybe it's because he looks so different now. Either way, I only give him a quick nod and then open the door.

CHAPTER FOUR

I pull my keys out of my pocket and start to unlock the truck when Mallory stops me.

"No, let's walk. Like we used to."

"Walk? Where?"

She raises her eyebrows, but I'm still amped from defying my dad. Unable to shake the electricity of leaving. She hits me and says, "The bridge, stupid. Where else are we going to go?"

It's not far, a mile or so, but walking feels too slow. A brake to our momentum. I want to go fast, to put an exclamation point on what just happened.

"But we'll get there faster if we drive," I say, opening

the truck. She comes over and closes the door gently, nodding toward the road, the bridge. Before she starts walking, ignoring the fact that I still haven't moved, she says,
"C'mon, it will be fun." It's not until she's a good fifty feet
away that I jog to her.

"That's what I thought," she says, smiling tentatively.
There's a cautious familiarity with her tone, an invitation
to jump back into our old skins when nothing was off-
limits, when everything was engaged passionately.
Everything was intimate. But like anything that's been
shed, what used to fit is now tight.

The untailored silence carries us until we're at the edge
of the train tracks, the embankment nothing but dirt and a
few roots poking through the ground. I lower myself down
and offer my hand to Mallory.

She ignores it and jumps down.

As soon as her feet hit, she immediately walks to the
far side of the bridge, scanning the ground, searching for
something. After a few seconds she yelps with excitement
and drops to her knees, digging into the ground with a
rock. When she turns around to face me, twin circles of
dirt on her knees and a coffee can in her hands, it catches
me like a punch.

"Holy shit," I say.

"I know."

"Are you sure that's it?"

She opens the lid, and a tiny puff of dust rises between us.

"Oh, yeah."

She pulls out what looks like a switchblade before hitting a button to reveal a comb instead of a knife. "Somebody went to Myrtle Beach. Yours, of course." She tosses it to me, and I turn the metal kitsch over in my hands. I got it, along with a shark tooth chain necklace, the summer of fourth grade and couldn't be found anywhere without either. We'd go to the grocery store, and I'd switch it open and run it through my hair. At school, open and through the hair. I would give it a swipe now except the bristles are caked with grime.

Mallory smiles quickly before looking back into the can.

"Ugh, remember this genius idea?" she says, pulling out a single Twinkie and tossing it toward me. I jump back, laughing. When it hits the ground, the package splits but the cake barely moves. "'They last *forever*, Mallory:' that's what you said."

"I remember," I say, bending down to investigate. The Twinkie isn't rancid or, honestly, even misshapen after all these years. It is decidedly a Twinkie. A disturbing shade of gray, yes, but a Twinkie still.

"I was right!"

"Oh, my God, don't be an idiot," she says.

"Look at it! It's still whole."

"Well, I'll let you have the first bite," she says, turning her attention back to the can.

I come closer to Mallory, looking over her shoulder as she digs. I can't deny the excitement. We buried this the summer before fifth grade. It was raining, and neither of us wanted to be stuck at home. When she showed up with the old Folgers can and told me we were leaving a time capsule for future Thomas and Mallory, I always figured we'd dig it up a couple of weeks later. On the next rainy day.

"Get in on this nostalgia," she says, handing me the can.

A couple of plastic rings, a collection of old movie tickets, faded and unreadable, a few train-flattened pennies. In the bottom, curled up around the inside of the can, a purple notebook.

It sends a shock through me. I pull the notebook out and open it. Mallory's loopy cursive is like a time machine. The first page is a map from each of our houses to the bridge, with "meet me here" written across the top. As if either of us would ever forget how to get to the bridge. The next page is a long letter, unsent, to a professional wrestler we both admired, Randy "The Beefcake" Simpson. The rest of it is just as random.

"I forgot about this," I say.

"'The Book of Adventures,'" she says, pointing to a flash of silver writing on the dark purple cover. "'And Other Miscellany,' obviously."

I close the notebook. "We were really lame."

I mean it to be endearing, but it sounds dismissive. As if I want to minimize what stuff like this meant. Mallory pulls out a plastic ring—purple, with flowers—and slips it onto her pinkie.

"I don't know," she says, studying the ring. "We seemed pretty cool to me."

She's smiling, the way she always would when we were younger. Big and goofy, like she just won a prize at one of the fly-by-night carnivals that appeared in the empty lot next to SuperMart overnight, disappearing just as suddenly a week later. She waits a moment before putting the ring back in the can.

Then she looks at me and says, "Why did you do it?"

My stomach clenches. I could play stupid. As if I didn't know exactly what she meant.

The last day of summer, just before sixth grade. We were going to different schools for the first time that year, and I was sick about it. She had planned one last hurrah, and the instructions showed up on my windowsill in typical Mallory fashion. A map adorned with princesses riding unicorns, all of it done in ironic pink and purple marker. I had a packing list, a destination. We were going to do what every kid in our small town had boasted and threatened to do since the beginning of time: sneak through the legendary fifteenth-floor door of the haunted Grover Hotel. The one with the warnings. The one that surely hid the kinds of horrors we'd internalized from every scary movie we'd ever seen.

"I didn't want to stop being your friend," I say.

She picks through the can without looking at me. "Okay. But I want to know."

"I can't remember. It was a long time ago."

Her face drops because it's bullshit, and we both know

it. I struggle to find the words because the truth still hurts. It feels like a betrayal, even now.

Of course I was going to meet her that afternoon. She called, I went. That's how it worked. I was getting a head-lamp from the garage when Dad came up behind me, the map in his hands. He held it like it was a dirty magazine, pinched between his finger and thumb.

The conversation was quick, over before I could say two words.

I was almost a man, and I needed to start acting like it. No more make-believe. No more running around with pink and purple maps in my pocket. No more Mallory. Of course he never said I couldn't be friends with her—not directly. But I understood. If I wanted to be like him and Jake—every man in my life—it had to start right then, no questions.

So I didn't go. For the first time ever. I didn't respond to her phone calls or to the knocks at the door. Being at a new school made the separation final. But right now, standing in front of her, I've never felt as ashamed.

The first time I saw her in high school, every reflex inside me angled toward her as if no time had passed. I walked up to her in the cafeteria and stood there, hoping she'd say something, grant absolution. Her new friends didn't know me, so I was just another awkward freshman. Their laughter was loud and embarrassing, and I split. A week went by, followed by four long years, neither of us making a move in the other's direction. And the longer I'm standing here, her eyes on me, the more I realize how stupid that was.

"You know how Dad is," I finally say.

"I do."

"It's his way or nothing. 'Gotta be a man, Thomas. Can't be seen around town like that, Thomas.' I didn't know what else to do. He found your note, and he told me I couldn't go. . . . Do you know what it's like to have somebody expect so much from you when you're not ready?"

She wipes at her eyes quickly, nodding. "Yes."

I hold on to the can like it's a life preserver and I'm stuck in the middle of the ocean.

"Basically I'm trying to say—"

She wipes her eyes one more time. "That you're kind of an asshole?"

"I mean, I was eleven."

"Still."

"Would you call an eleven-year-old an asshole?" I ask.

"Well, probably. But I'm not the best example of good behavior these days." She halfheartedly throws a punch. I look at the ground, trying to will up the courage to actually apologize. Because as always, I can't stand up for anything.

"I wish I wouldn't have listened to him, if that matters."

"It does," she says, her eyes drifting back to the inside of the can.

"And I'm sorry," I say, but Mallory tries to wave it away. I take the can from her and force eye contact. "No, really. I was the biggest eleven-year-old asshole, ever."

It makes her laugh, the sound echoing off the concrete walls of the bridge. "You should put that on a T-shirt. I'm sure they'd love that in the army."

She gives me a stiff salute, clicking her heels together and everything. I try to hide the way my body goes rigid.

Would I have told her? Surely. And right now that feels like a bit of grace. She doesn't have to be burdened by this, too. Instead, she'll learn, just like the rest of the town, that I'm nothing like my brother, my father. That I'm a fraud.

I shake the can and say, "You should keep this. Do some of these things with Will."

She pulls off the ring and drops it in the can and then

rolls up the notebook and stuffs it back inside. Then she says, "Yeah. Maybe I will."

She walks a step behind me, neither of us saying much as we cross the field and walk back up Plateau Road toward my house. Every few minutes a car comes flying by. One honks, another flashes its lights, and we both stop, turning around to see an older couple shaking their heads disapprovingly. When we get to the entrance of my neighborhood, the manufactured houses set off in the distance in precisely placed rows, Mallory stops walking. She looks serious as hell, her eyes focused on me like I might sprint away. Like she'll need to give chase. Without saying anything else, she opens the can and pulls out the notebook.

"What are you doing?" I ask, and she shushes me, flipping through the decorated pages of the notebook. When she finally finds what she's looking for, she holds it close to her chest.

"What if I said you could apologize to me *and* right all of your past transgressions in one teensy little hour?"

"I'd say you have no idea what time I'm getting up in the morning."

She hits me with the notebook.

"You really piss me off, Bennett. I'm trying to get you to take me to the Grover, but you're like some preprogrammed computer. 'Must Go Home. Fun does not compute.' "

She tilts her body like a robot as she talks. When I don't respond, she sighs and pushes the notebook toward me. It's a list, one hundred reasons never to go to the Grover Hotel by Mallory and Thomas, age nine and three-quarters. I skim the rest of the pages: unicorns, a halfhearted ninja. Each page is a flip-book of Mallory. I stare at the notebook for another second before I hand it back to her.

"Any other night and I'd go," I say.

She smiles faintly and nods a couple of times. "You're right, sorry. You've got a lot going on, I just thought it would be fun. But hey, at least I've got this, right?" She shakes the can once before putting it back under her arm. "Give me a ride home at least?"

As we walk toward my house, I wait for her to bring the full-court pressure. To come up with 101 Reasons Why Thomas Is Dumb and Boring and how it's impossible for me to resist her plan, the magic words that got me so many times before. But she doesn't say anything, just walks next to me, expressionless but not upset, in the summer night.

My house is still lit up, and I see Mom and Dad yelling at each other before I hear them. Dad's pointing toward the living room, where Jake sits unmoving on the couch, the backpack on his lap. Mom has her face in her hands, and when Dad tries to pull them away, she shakes loose and runs to their bedroom. It's impossible that Mallory didn't see it, didn't hear the words coming loud and emphatic from my dad's mouth.

"He's fine."

We're standing at the top of the driveway, and they can't see us, have no idea that we're watching or listening. Most of the time, when they've argued about Jake—whether he needs help or what that even means—it floats through the thin walls of our house, coming to me as invisible words. I never saw Mom crying or Dad sitting at the table, like he is now, reading the paper like nothing's wrong.

I run down the driveway, get in the truck, and start the engine. Dad squints out the window, stands up, but I've already backed up to Mallory. I've got the door open when he comes out, calling my name. At first she doesn't get in, her face shocked and confused and, maybe, excited. I have no idea how to explain the desperation, the pain. How badly I need her to get in the truck right now so I don't have to talk to my dad, so I don't have to pretend again—like always—that Jake is fine.

When Mallory takes a step toward the truck, Dad says her name, but she's already in the seat and buckled before he's taken three steps.

I put the truck in gear, and then we're gone.

CHAPTER FIVE

When we were kids, the Grover was still an operational hotel, and none of us could keep ourselves out of its hallways. I didn't know a kid who hadn't been kicked out at least once. As we grew, so did the legends. In third grade, it was haunted—lousy with ghosts. In fourth, I firmly believed it when Wallace David reported an entire family was murdered on the top floor. Even last year, I heard a couple of sophomores telling their friends it had been transformed into the headquarters for a motorcycle club's drug operation. But no matter the rumor, everything happened on the fifteenth floor, the only floor in the hotel that didn't allow guests. It wouldn't have been strange if it had been the top floor. But there were twenty-five stories in the Grover. No explanation, just nailed shut with a warning: ANYONE WHO OPENS THIS DOOR WILL BE ARRESTED IMMEDIATELY.

It begged elementary theories, for which we were the perfect age.

I'm pushing ten, fifteen over the speed limit before I start to feel what happened, the shit that's going to fall on me whenever I go back home. Mallory doesn't say anything as I skid around another corner. In the distance a halo of white streetlights circles the otherwise dark sky.

Mallory is going through my glove compartment, trying her best to keep things light. "You don't know how long I've waited for this. The Grover. Do you have a flashlight in here?"

"No," I say.

"Shit's going to be *dark*."

"Maybe we should just go somewhere else," I say. She stops bouncing and gives me a look, like I'm a punk and she just figured it out.

"Somewhere else? Are you high?"

When she turns to face me, the levity disappears

momentarily. She leans closer, as if she were inspecting a piece of fruit.

"I'm officially about to take this night to the next level." I try to say something, and she holds up her hand. "*Next level.*"

"Listen, I just wanted to get away from my house. Maybe we could drive by and then go get something to eat. At the Waffle House."

"I'm talking about the Grover, the fifteenth floor, and you counter with . . . the Waffle House? Man up, Bennett. *Man up.*"

Her phone goes off, and we both jump. She checks the screen, rolls her eyes, and shoves the phone back into her shorts. All the confidence escapes her.

"Will?" I ask.

She nods, trying to play off the anxiety that's gripping her face. "Whatever. We're going to the Grover."

"It's not like you don't have things going on, too," I say. "We can do this some other time."

She tries to work herself back up, to force enthusiasm as the phone rings again in her pocket. "Look, Bennett. You're not the only one who needs a distraction tonight. All I want for graduation is to go to the Grover."

She lets that hang there, not saying anything else, then opens the glove compartment again. "Now, do you have a flashlight or not?"

"There's a full moon," I say.

"Oh, shit, you're right. I didn't think about were-wolves." I sigh, and she laughs. "Don't worry, I brought the silver bullets."

It takes ten minutes to get to the Grover, and when I make the last turn onto the dark street, the building leans over us. As I roll to a stop, Mallory's phone goes off again, but she ignores it. She's out of the truck and over the fence before I can close my door. When I catch up, she laces her fingers through the links on the fence, facing me.

"Well, c'mon." Her voice is soft, excited.

I look up at the hotel. Every reason not to do this is now rising up like tiny flares.

"It's got a fence around it for a reason," I say.

"Thomas, there's not really ghosts in there—just so you know."

"I'm more worried about tetanus from a nail. It's dark as hell in there."

"If you get tetanus, I'll suck the poison out of the wound for you."

"That doesn't make sense."

"I'll carry you to the hospital, crying, screaming out your name as I burst through the ER doors."

"This is all really helpful, but—"

She rattles the fence. "But what? If you can give me one good reason not to go into the Grover, I swear to God we can leave and I'll never speak of it again."

Her head cocks to the side before she turns around, not bothering to wait for my answer, and begins searching for a way into the building. From over her shoulder she says: "I'm going in. Stay out here if you want, but know that it's weak."

She boosts herself on top of a Dumpster and then uses every inch of her height to push open a cracked window. She climbs up the wall and disappears into the hotel.

I look down the street, assuring myself that I'm no longer swayed by what Mallory thinks about me. I'll sit out here and wait on the curb until she realizes this is stupid and then—what? I don't want to go home, not yet. But what else could we possibly do tonight?

One minute goes by, two. When my phone goes off, I pull it out. I'm sure she's stuck in rotting floorboards. But it's my mom. I hesitate before putting it back in my pocket.

"Mallory?"

Nothing. I say her name again, but the only sound is a car somewhere in the distance. When I put my foot on the fence, I'm already cussing myself because damn it, I know better.

When I drop into the hotel, she looks proud—of me or the fact that we're finally standing in the Grover. She spreads her arms wide, presenting the lobby, which smells like damp paper and campfires. Its walls are tagged with graffiti; an impressive rocket ship—it might be a penis—climbs into the darkness of the stairway. What furniture remains is scattered around the room, fighting for space on the floor with a diverse collection of half-empty beer bottles.

It's the stairway that catches our attention, though.

"Well, let's do this," she says, taking a step toward the stairs. We climb together, and it doesn't take long for the darkness to become problematic. Even with the lights from our phones, I step on the back of Mallory's foot and try to catch myself on a handrail that isn't there. When I stumble against the wall, she laughs.

"Do you need to hold my hand? We can make a train."

Images of elementary school, of walking hand in hand

like living paper dolls, come to me in the darkness. I reach out and feel along the peeled walls of the hotel. Two turns later, a slant of moonlight appears through a dusty window one story above us. Mallory stops and glances back at me.

"We stayed here once when our house flooded," she says.

"I remember," I say. We tried to get my parents to let her stay at my house for the week, but Dad didn't think it was appropriate having a girl share my room, even if we were nine and only interested in staying up late to talk and sneak some television.

"We stayed on the next floor." She continues. "My parents wouldn't let me go anywhere alone, or I would've already done this."

"Yeah, okay," I say. She stops, offended.

"I would've gone to the fifteenth floor. Believe that."

She stands there, hands on hips, waiting for me to say I believe her. But hell, no. There's no way she would've opened that door. That's the whole point. That's why we're here right now. And besides, I have proof.

"Fifth grade."

It takes a second, but the recognition comes. Suddenly she's really interested in making it up the next eight flights of stairs.

"Where are you going?" I ask.

"I don't have all night. We have to make this happen."

"But I thought we were having a good conversation. Reminiscing, all that."

"Screw you, Bennett," she says.

I smile and follow her up the stairs. The first time we were supposed to do this, before I ruined everything—still our fifth-grade year—she canceled. She had an excuse, of course—her mom needed her to go grocery shopping or something—but it was a high-water mark. The one time Mallory shied away from anything, at least as far as I know.

I haven't been counting the flights, so when we get to the landing—just the same as every other one we've passed, minus the actual hallways leading to the rooms—we stand there in a semi-stunned silence.

"It's not boarded up," she says. "That's weird, right? I feel like it should be boarded up."

I look at the door, the infamous sign. It doesn't look ominous, just a door in a hotel. Mallory doesn't move, almost paralyzed by being this close. Without thinking, I reach out and grab the doorknob. It swings open easily, as if it had never been locked. Neither of us moves.

Large windows bring in plenty of light, but that's not
the problem. There's nothing here. The whole floor, really
just a big room, is almost empty. It spans the entire width
and length of the hotel. Forgotten paint cans are scattered
around the room, as if somebody were trying to compare a
hundred different shades of beige, along with broken legs
from dining room tables and a few disassembled luggage
carts.

"Oh hell no." Mallory steps past me and into the empty
room. "My whole life I was told there were ghosts or mur-
derers—satanists, at least—living up here. And it's just an
attic?"

"I never heard about the satanists," I say.

She turns around and looks at me. "Really? Hmm. Well,
it doesn't matter, obviously. Our entire childhood was a
sham because look . . ." She swipes an arm around the
room. In the distance I can make out something: chairs,
maybe an old bed frame. We walk around the perimeter
of the room, touching the walls and bending over when
something glints in the moonlight. In one corner Mallory
finds an old sleeping bag and an empty bottle of Boone's
Farm wine. She holds it up and says, "Satanists."

When we get back to the door, Mallory stops and says,

"Well, this was a huge disappointment."

I'm looking around the room; even in the hotel's heyday, I can't imagine they used this to store anything exceptionally valuable. Maybe a few televisions, some minirefrigerators. So while it's disappointing to know that all the rumors were never true, I can't get past one thing.

"Why the sign?" I ask.

"Because they knew this day would come and they wanted to ruin our childhood," Mallory says.

"Okay, but besides that. Why in the hell would they put up a sign like that if it's empty?"

Mallory thinks for a second. "Right! Why not put up a sign that says EMPLOYEES ONLY?"

"Or nothing. No sign. Then who even cares about going through that door?"

She shakes her head angrily. "Screw this. I'm getting my memory."

She walks over to the door, carefully sliding her fingers underneath the edges of the sign. It's made of sheet metal and, on better days, would be impossible to remove from the door. But now the screws are brown with rust, and she pulls it off with little effort.

She holds it up victorious. As if we'd just solved one of

life's greatest mysteries—found Bigfoot. When she gives me the sign, the metal is weightless and cool in my hand. It's just a sign, something an eighteen-year-old shouldn't find captivating. But as I turn it over, I'm not sure I've ever missed our friendship more.

CHAPTER SIX

I want to rush down the stairs, refusing to let the excitement of the adventure drain out of the night. But Mallory moves without urgency, so I slow myself, trying to put my feet in the tracks she leaves in the dust, the rectangular sign getting warm in my hand.

"Well, we're officially felons," I say.

"Or heroes," she says, her voice filled with an excited manic energy. "Speaking of that . . . Jake. He looked . . . rough."

It takes a floor before I answer her. The silence is heavy, choking me. Calling Jake rough is gracious. I swallow once and say, "They're naming a bridge after him."

She stops, holding her cell phone up so I can see her face. "What? Which one?"

"River Road. Down near Highway Ten."

When Jake came home, my dad said he was a little off. *Off.* It implied that he could be fixed by flipping a switch, that with time, he'd be back on. The old Jake again. So I covered up for him, every day and no matter what. People ask and I tell them he's doing well. I tell them about the bridge and getting to meet the president. About the medals, even though I found them in the garbage can a few weeks after he came home. He didn't have an answer for that, of course, so I put them in my room, under my bed, next to old video games and a forgotten baseball card collection. But he isn't getting better. He sits there all day with that backpack, rarely talking or changing clothes. He's a constant presence that's not really there.

"The Jake Bennett Bridge," Mallory says. "That's impressive. Seriously. I know a few guys who would give their left nut to have a bridge named after them."

I mumble a "yeah," and Mallory gives me a puzzled look. I don't want to let the air out of our accomplishment, but I can't properly explain my feelings about the bridge.

At least not without giving away everything. I hit the sign with my knuckle lightly.

"This is pretty badass," I say.

She raises her eyebrows and nods, leading us down the rest of the stairs until we reach the lobby. As soon as we are off the stairs, a white light cuts through the darkness. It animates the dark lobby, bringing life to the shadows. Dust floats across the room lazily, an entire invisible world. And then a voice comes from outside, amplified by a speaker.

"I know you're in there. So come on out."

Mallory looks at the faded warnings written on the sign and then at me. "Damn. They weren't kidding about the fifteenth floor." She squints into the light, holding her hand above her eyes. Past the light I can see the outlines of a police car. The officer stands behind the cruiser's door, the mic pressed to his lips.

"C'mon now. I can see you through the glass."

"I say we hide," Mallory says dramatically. "We could live inside the Grover forever. They'd never find us."

This is the way she always played, like we'd never get caught, no matter the scheme. She was always fantastical, and I was there to force us back to reality. Right now I wish I believed we could disappear inside this hotel and nobody would come looking. But a police officer is about as real as it gets. I can already see the newspaper tomorrow morning: LOCAL HERO'S BROTHER BARRICADES SELF IN ABANDONED HOTEL.

When I start for the front door, Mallory doesn't look disappointed or even surprised. "Just hold up a second," she says as she carefully works the metal sign beneath the back of her shirt. As soon as she's finished, she looks over her left, then right shoulder and gives me a thumbs-up.

The officer studies our licenses and then our faces before he says, "What were you two doing in there?"

"We just graduated," Mallory says, acting as if she's not hiding a sign under her shirt.

The officer seems tired, like he's heard this reason too many times tonight. He gives our IDs one more glance before handing Mallory's back to her. When I reach for mine, he pulls it back.

"Bennett. Like the kid from the papers? The soldier?"

"That's my brother," I say, taking my license from him.

"And you're going, too, right? I read that somewhere."

When Jake got back, a reporter came to the house

wanting to do another story. Like every other time before, Dad made Jake wear the dress blues. And of course the reporter ate it up. When he found out Dad was a bona fide hero, too, first on the ground in Desert Storm just days after Jake was born, not to mention me, headed in the same direction once I graduated, he got out a second notebook and spent the whole afternoon prying into every nook of our life. That Sunday Dad bought every copy at the gas station, smiling like we'd won the lottery.

Back then I still wanted to go. I would've killed for Jake to tell me his stories, the kind Dad had told at the dinner table when we were growing up. Stories about being a part of something bigger and greater than yourself. About bravery and sacrifice. Jake lived it, just like Dad. Maybe more so. Because when he got injured saving those two soldiers, there wasn't a question about his claim to the title hero. And all I wanted was for him to impart even the smallest bit of truth, of wisdom to me.

"I ship tomorrow," I say.

He reaches for my hand, which is another thing people started doing once that article came out, pumping it up and down like I'm running for office.

"God bless you, son. If I was younger, I would've enlisted myself a few years back." He smiles, pulling me closer and forcing eye contact. "You give 'em hell for me, all right?"

"Yes, sir," I say.

He makes me promise him that we'll stay away from the Grover and gives me one last clap on the shoulder. As he drives away, Mallory looks visibly relieved. She pulls the sign out, wincing once, and then holds it for both of us to see.

"No wonder there's so much crime here. How did he not see this?"

She riffs on the state of law enforcement in our town, but I'm barely there. Barely listening.

"I'm surprised he didn't ask for your autograph," she says. "He was all 'Oh, you're a Bennett? I'm about to die from excitement.'"

"Yeah," I say.

I'm trying to smile, but I can't stop thinking about the way that police officer looked at me, like I'm doing him a personal favor by joining the army. It's ridiculous because what he thinks shouldn't matter. But the sense of disappointing him, this entire town, is something I can't shake.

Because who will I be if I don't follow in the Bennett footsteps?

"Let's go do something else," I say.

Mallory does a double take and knocks on my head. "Is that you in there, Thomas? I thought you were going to turn into a pumpkin if I didn't get you home soon."

"It's graduation," I say weakly.

She studies me for a moment, trying to guess my angle. Here's another chance to be straight with someone. And with such little risk. I could tell her, and poof, it's over. But sometimes it feels like I've forgotten how to be real with anyone. So I force a senior picture–worthy smile and say, "Give me the notebook."

She pulls it out of her back pocket and hands it to me, still watching my every move. I flip through the pages, one after the other, trying to make my face upbeat and normal. But everything on the page is ambiguous now. Ten-year-olds projecting their idea of cool into the future.

The frustration cakes my voice. "Maybe we could just drive around. I don't know."

She takes the notebook when I hand it back to her, still watching me. "Yeah, Thomas. We can do that."

· · ·

Mallory holds the notebook on her lap with one hand; the other she hangs out the window, letting the wind lift and drop it. The only sound is the rustling of the notebook's pages, our childhood blowing in the wind.

I'd drive until the sun came up and went down again if I thought I could get away with it, letting the radio mute whatever I was feeling. The wind would blow away all my problems. Jake, my dad, all of it would disappear if only I drove long enough. But when I hit Plateau Road, when I can see Ford High School looming in the distance, reality hits me in the gut.

The teachers, my friends, people I'll never meet. Everyone expects something I can't give them, expects me to be this person that I've fraudulently created. The weight of all of them pushes on my chest, and I begin to panic.

I need to get out of this town.

But that means going home and taking the yelling, the shocked disbelief. It's swallowing everything for a few more hours, once again turning the disappointment into a tank of fuel, a reason to get me on the road.

And I don't know if I can do that either.

Then there's Mallory. No matter the nostalgia, the weightlessness of being out with her, it has to end. If the past few months with Jake have taught me anything, it's that ignoring facts does not transform them. Fact: I cannot go to the army tomorrow. Fact: I cannot tell anyone. And that leaves me with the last and final fact: The longer I'm out here with Mallory, the harder it becomes to get away.

I can barely breathe when I make a hard right into Ford's parking lot. Mallory curses as she grabs for the door. I stop the truck just around the corner from the football field and put it in park.

"What the hell, Thomas!" Mallory reaches down and picks up the notebook. When she actually sees my face, she says, "Are you okay?"

"I need to explain something to you," I say.

I search for the words, something that will honor what we've done tonight but will also make it clear that what's happening right now has to end. If I don't leave—and soon—I'm not sure what will happen. But I want her to know that we can build from here. When I come home, we can try this again. It just can't be tonight.

I try to breathe, but every breath is hard and ragged.

Mallory stares at me waiting. But I'm afraid if I open my mouth, I'm going to have to tell another lie. And I can't do it. Not anymore. I fall back into my seat exhausted.

"Is this because of Jake?" she asks. I nod, and she starts to say something but stops herself. Then, quickly, she says, "He's kind of screwed up, right? I mean, I heard things, people saying he was weird now. But people can be assholes, so—"

I've gotten so good at being quiet, at keeping my emotions in check. But when she reaches over and puts her hand on mine, says my name, it's like a river coming over the banks. The words slip from my mouth like a secret.

"He is so messed up," I say. "All he does is sit at the house and watch videos on the computer and eat frozen pizzas and—"

This is where I usually shut it down. Once, at school, a teacher asked, and I got this far before I started zippering everything closed. My mouth, all the feelings, the fear. Shutting down works because nobody pays attention, not really. For most people, Jake can be both hero and recluse because in that world nobody has to care except for me.

"Is it because he got shot?" she asks.

"Honestly, I don't know," I say. "The other night I had to go pick him up because he was halfway to Sherrills Ford. That's like twenty miles away, and he was *walking*. For no reason."

I drop my head. Even now I can't say it out loud. The only words anyone ever uses—*crazy, sick, off*—don't capture what's wrong with Jake.

Mallory leans closer to me. "Hey, he's going to be fine."

"I don't think he is."

As soon as I say it, I'm nervous. If Mallory has a reaction, she doesn't show it. I can't tell if she doesn't know what to say or maybe she can't believe I'd betray Jake, everybody's hero, so easily.

"I'm really sorry," she says, not looking up.

I thank her quietly. The awkwardness begins filling up the truck by the bucketful until the unmistakable sound of a shotgun discharging rings across the night, immediately followed by shattering glass and enthusiastic male catcalls.

All I can think is: thank God for Hickory, North Carolina.

Voices dart across the empty parking lot, around the buildings. The words are muddled nonsense.

I start my truck because who knows how many beers these guys finished before the firearms came out. Before I can put the truck in gear, Mallory says, "So I'm guessing that's what your parents were arguing about."

I let the truck idle, hoping for another shotgun blast.

But nothing comes, so I nod my head. "Of course. Dad says: 'Jake is tough. Jake's a man. He just needs some time to get right.'"

"What does your mom think?"

"That cookies and cake will solve all the problems."

"I'm sure she sees it."

"I see it," I say. "But what does it matter if nobody does anything about it?"

It sounds harsher than I intend, weeks and months of frustration coming at her like shards of glass. When her phone goes off, she stares at me for three rings before punching the button and lifting it to her ear. The one-sided conversation is loud and angry.

"Well, stop calling then . . . Why do you care? . . . Fine, you want to know? I'm with Thomas . . . Yes . . . Yeah, we're making sweet, mad love, Will—what do you think? . . . Okay, I'm hanging up now."

This time it's Mallory who goes quiet. She stares at the notebook still in her lap. We could've been sitting there for a hundred years before she says, "All I'm saying is, maybe your parents have reasons for what they're doing . . . or not doing."

"Ho-ly *shit*. Sin, will you look at this?"

Wayne Lewis is standing in front of my truck, holding a shotgun and nodding to Sinclair Williams. I've known them both since kindergarten. Good friends, but the sort of guys who only know how to have fun that ends with the police showing up.

Wayne squints into the truck. "Oh man, Thomas. Did we just ruin your graduation hookup?"

Mallory opens the door and waves. When the light catches her face and Wayne sees her, he smiles. "Might need to reload this twelve gauge, Sin. This boy right here's in need of protection, messing around with another man's woman."

I'm about to tell Wayne we're leaving, when Mallory gets out of the truck and points at the shotgun. "Hey, can I get a go with that?"

Wayne looks more surprised than I do, and for the next ten minutes I couldn't tell Mallory and Wayne the world was ending, let alone try to get either of them to disengage. Wayne is impressed and fascinated that a girl would want to stand on the back of his pickup and fire a shotgun at empty beer bottles. He shows her how to hold the gun against her shoulder, how to trace the bottles Sinclair throws across the parking lot. Her phone goes off inside the cab of my truck, but if she hears it, I can't tell.

"All right, get ready for this," Wayne says, motioning to Sinclair.

The bottle goes airborne, and she misses it completely, rubbing her shoulder and cursing from the kickback. Wayne still cups his hands and lets out his best yell.

"Damn. That *hurt*," Mallory says, still rubbing her shoulder.

"Nice shot," I say.

She turns to me, a challenge in her eyes. "You think you can do better?"

Dad taught me to shoot years ago, and Wayne's twelve gauge isn't any different from the one in Dad's gun safe. But I also know Wayne. A couple of shotgun blasts could easily turn into our spending the next seven hours sitting in the back of his truck, drinking beer and listening to his stories. We'd be here until dawn.

"Okay, soldier boy," Wayne says, holding the gun out to me. "Let's see what you've got."

"I'm not getting caught shooting a gun in the parking lot of a school," I say.

Wayne and Sinclair consider the felonious nature of this statement briefly before laying into me. Asking if I need to go home for some quiet time. Whether my yoga practice is affecting my trigger finger. All that.

"How is that vegan diet?" Wayne asks.

I still haven't moved when Mallory takes the gun from Wayne and says, "Sinclair, throw another bottle." And this time it doesn't get twenty feet from Sinclair's hand before it explodes, raining glass everywhere.

"Hot damn!" Wayne nearly falls off the back of his truck with excitement. But she's already jumping off the bed and walking to me, a taunt etched into her face and the shotgun in her hands.

"One shot and nobody will think you're a punk."

"You must have me confused with somebody else."

"Somebody who's a punk?"

"I think I've got a slingshot in the truck!" Sinclair laughs as he says it. I hesitate a second too long.

"I understand if you're scared," Mallory yells, for the world to hear. "Especially now that I've shown what's *what*."

"Hitting one is easy," I say. "Anybody can do that. You hit two, three in a row? Then maybe I'm impressed."

Mallory takes the challenge, eyeing me as she lifts the gun to her shoulder. She misses the next three bottles, each one smashing against the parking lot. At first she doesn't look at me, just stands there for a second contemplating what she's going to say next.

"Well, if you don't shoot, you're still a punk," she says, handing the gun to Wayne.

It gets a hallelujah chorus from the idiots as Mallory scans me up and down, like "Let's see what you can do." If I don't shoot, nothing happens. Maybe they give me hell for another fifteen minutes, and probably not even that long. But if I do shoot, if I miss I'll never hear the end of it.

But I don't think I'll miss. Having a stock against my shoulder is like learning to ride a bike in most other families. You walk, you get a little age to you, you learn to shoot. BB guns, a hunting rifle: I've shot everything. As I'm going through all of this, I can't think of a good reason not to take the challenge. And besides, it will be nice to finally win something with Mallory. Even if it took eighteen years to make it happen.

When I stand up, Mallory starts clapping, throwing her hands up in the air like she's at church. Then she's in my ear, taunting me, whispered put-downs that are half-hearted at best. I climb into the truck bed, trying not to listen to her or Wayne and Sinclair's commentary on the state of my manhood as I reject the shotgun and pick up the .22 leaning against the truck instead.

"Throw three in a row," I say, checking the sight and getting a feeling for the weight of the gun in my hands. "After I hit the first, throw the second, then the third. Okay?"

"That's presumptuous," Mallory says, but I ignore her.

When I nod to Sinclair, everything stops moving for a second. The first bottle is in the air, and all I can hear is myself breathing as I pull the trigger. The second, the third: all of them are taken from the sky one after another. When I drop the barrel of the gun, everyone's silent for a second.

I smile as Mallory shakes her head, refusing to look at me.

"Well, at least I can rest easy knowing America's going to be safe," Wayne says, taking the gun and slapping me on the shoulder. "When do you leave, man?"

"Tomorrow," I say.

"Oh, shit! Tomorrow? Like, *tomorrow* tomorrow?"

"I'll be gone before the sun even comes up," I say.

"See, Sinclair, that's what I'm trying to tell you," Wayne says. "This right here is a man with plans. He's going to *war*, son."

"I'm not going to war," I say. Wayne and Sinclair both ignore me.

"You know I'm waiting on NASCAR to call," Sinclair says, adjusting his ball cap. "And just because you graduate from high school doesn't mean you're ready to go out and get a job. And *that's* why I'm staying with my parents this year. It's called a gap year, idiot."

Wayne stares at him for a long minute. "Sitting around your mom's basement getting high and playing Madden isn't a gap year. Hell, it's your senior year—just no school."

"Okay, fair enough," Sinclair says. "But it's not like I won't be working. I got a job up at Wagner Tires this summer."

"Yeah, yeah, enough with your *gap year*." Wayne turns to me. "So what are we doing?"

"Nothing," I say.

"Yeah, haven't you heard? He's *leaving in the morning*," Mallory deadpans.

"It's graduation night," Wayne says. "And hell if I'm not drinking a beer with you before you go. Sinclair, where's the next party?"

Sinclair pulls out a piece of paper from his back pocket, and before he can say anything, Mallory stops him.

"What is that?"

"List of all the graduation parties," Sinclair says. "Some are actually probably more get-togethers, but that's semantics. Anyway, we could go up to the quarry. There's some people going up there tonight."

Mallory throws her arm around Sinclair, both of them staring at me and nodding. "I love these guys. We're in."

"Hell, yes," Wayne says, shouldering the .22. "We're about two moments away from jail right now, and we need a good influence. Somebody with moral fiber to put us on the right path."

"Oh, that's Thomas," Mallory says. "Full of moral fiber."

"I don't want to go to a party," I say.

"It's not a party," Mallory says. "It's a *get-together*. Weren't you listening?"

"Yeah, Sin's really particular about that shit, too."

Sinclair sighs, putting the list back in his pocket. "A party's bigger, there's an expectation that you stay longer. See more people. A get-together is casual."

"Hear that? Sounds *exactly* like what you need tonight," Mallory says. For a second her face softens and she raises her eyebrows a half inch. "You know?"

Wayne doesn't give me a chance to answer. He slaps me on the shoulder and says, "We're going to the quarry, end of story. You're officially occupied, Bennett. Sin, get the truck."

And just like that, we're four.

CHAPTER SEVEN

The quarry is for drinking beer, building a fire with friends. It's whooping and hollering and stumbling into the dark corners with your boyfriend or girlfriend. And then somebody decides to jump into the lake fifty feet below and everybody packs it up until the next weekend. I've done this dozens of times by now and more than a few with Wayne and Sinclair. But never with Mallory.

Maybe that's why it's so quiet in the truck. I'm following Wayne to the quarry, trying to conjure up the magic of the Grover and, to a smaller extent, the parking lot. In those moments I don't think about Jake or the army. I don't think about how I've missed Mom's curfew now or how every minute I spend out with Mallory is a minute I'm not sleeping in preparation for the trip.

"Look at you," Mallory says. "Like you're going to a funeral."

Her phone rings, and she silences it without looking. Ahead of us Wayne turns onto a gravel road, the dark trees camouflaging everything except the twin brake lights that flash on and off as he navigates the narrow road.

"We should've come up here before this," she says. "And how did we not put it in the 'Book of Adventures'?"

I laugh. "I'm pretty sure drinking beer around a campfire wasn't high on our priorities back then. But yeah, I know."

We park behind Wayne, the small dirt clearing packed full of vehicles. A fire is already burning. Shadows crawl up and down the rock walls. This isn't a get-together. It's a party and a big one.

I take a few breaths, readying myself for what's coming. People will ask about tomorrow, and I'll smile, tell them I can't wait to get that uniform on. Everybody around this fire has known me since we were kids, and I've already been lying to them without pause for months. But the prospect of doing it even one more time makes my stomach drop.

Mallory's phone goes off, followed by mine: Mom. I hesitate before putting my phone in the cup holder. Outside, the group greets Wayne's arrival with a cheer, a few of them standing up and slapping him on the shoulder. He and Sinclair grab a beer and raise them in the air.

"You okay?" Mallory asks.

"Yeah, I'm good."

"Okay, because I need some more memories," Mallory says, pulling the sign out.

"What are you doing?" But she's already out of the truck, holding it above her head and whooping like some kind of deranged cheerleader. People yell because they're buzzing, but it gets louder and louder as people start to realize exactly what she's holding. They're so enamored with the sign nobody notices me walk up.

"Fifteenth floor, *what*?" Mallory says, pulling me toward her. "Luckily I had soldier boy here to keep me safe."

They pass the sign around the campfire, telling their own stories, the rumors that all share a little piece of truth. When somebody finally asks what was up there, Mallory doesn't say anything. She turns to me, and at first I don't realize she wants me to take over, to explain.

"Satanists," I say, trying to hide my smile when they all stop talking, moving. One of them, Emma West, nods her head knowingly and thrusts her beer to the sky, yelling out, "Satanists!" And then everybody cheers.

Wayne ambles through the group, handing me and Mallory each a beer. When the sign makes its way back to Mallory, I think I'm clear. I'll be able to sit here like any other guy in our class; the only difference is that I'll pretend to drink the beer because the last thing I need is to be hung over tomorrow morning. But then Wayne goes into the middle of the circle, clinking his bottle against his belt buckle.

"The United States Army has obviously lowered their standards," he says to the group. They all laugh. Most of them are going to college; none of their parents want them anywhere near the army, even if the chance of active duty is remote. They don't want heroes, just happiness.

"But we know all about Thomas Bennett, don't we? This is the guy who once put deodorant on the outside of his shirt for the sixth-grade choir concert, because he didn't know how it worked." Laughter. They want to send me off right. And every word that Wayne speaks gets them going more, which I appreciate. But I also wish he'd just raise his beer already and stop. Of course he keeps going. "The kid who used to wear camouflage to all the junior high dances, which now that I think about it is pretty genius. Respect, Bennett."

Wayne walks over to me, wrapping a thick arm around my shoulders. "Raise your beers to Thomas, y'all. May he go and kill a bunch of terrorists!"

As people stand and tilt their beers back in my honor, Mallory leans close and says, "Eloquent and subtle as always."

The firelight slaps against the walls of the quarry, distorting our shadows until we're all taller than the trees— giants in the darkness. It's how I always expected to feel on this night: big enough to take on anything.

Somebody turns on a car stereo and opens the doors. A few people start dancing as the music fills the night. Mallory leans over to me, and at first I think she's going to ask me to dance. My whole body goes tight.

"Despite everything, I'm glad this is happening."

"Me, too," I say.

She nods and stares into the fire, taking short sips from her beer. Eventually she puts it down and sits on one of the empty logs. I sit down next to her as we watch everybody dance and laugh around the fire. We're still sitting that way when Daniel walks up, wanting to chat me up. He hoped to sign up for the marines but won't turn eighteen for another two months, and his parents wouldn't sign the papers. Then he got into Appalachian State, and last I heard he was going to major in business.

I have to stand to hear him, and Mallory drifts off to another group. As Daniel complains about his parents, I watch Mallory smile at whatever Wayne is saying to her.

"So I bet you're excited," he says, sucking the last drops of beer from his bottle before throwing it over the edge of the quarry. "Do you think you'll go overseas?"

"I don't know, man. I'll probably end up in Kansas."

"Fucking Kansas," Daniel says.

I keep the conversation going with as few words as possible until Mallory comes up next to me and knocks me with her hip.

"Hey, mind if I steal this guy for a minute?"

"Oh, yeah. Sure. Hey, where's Will?"

But we're already turning around and walking away from the fire. She leads me past another group, all of them too interested in their conversation to notice us as we squeeze around them. I follow her up a narrow path, through the thick woods. Soon I can't see the fire below us. Mallory continues to climb until we break through the trees to a small collection of boulders. She sits down and pats the rock next to her.

"Will and I come up here," she says, once I'm sitting down.

"Oh, I don't want to know about that."

She shakes her head. "To talk, stupid. Look." Below us, in the valley, lights pulse on and off like they're on timers. She points to the brightest cluster and says, "That's downtown, and over there is your house. You can see the whole town up here."

The lights seem to move below us, a map of colors that make the city look prettier than it has ever been. The way I always remember Christmas when I was a kid.

"I thought you'd like to see where we grew up before you leave," Mallory says.

"It's very . . . peaceful."

She thinks I'm kidding and hits me in the arm. But I'm not. The sky is more open here—even more than where Wayne and the rest of them are laughing, not fifteen feet below. Above us, the stars fight against the city lights in the distance, seeming to grow brighter with every passing second until they form a blurry union, indistinguishable from one another.

"Do you think the stars look the same everywhere?" Mallory asks.

I have to think about it. "Sure. I mean, they have to, right?"

"So if you end up over there," she says carefully, "it'll be like you're looking at the stars in North Carolina?"

I nod, but I've done this enough to know what comes next, her plea for me to be careful, to choose myself over others—and I stop her.

"I'm not going anywhere overseas. At this point, unless you're Special Forces or something, it's back to normal."

"I just figured you'd volunteer, or something stupid like that." She pauses. "Are you scared?"

I nearly jump off the rock in surprise. I'm up, walking around the narrow boulder, trying to be calm, cool. But she's looking at me like I just set myself on fire. Before I decided to leave—to take fear off the table—I would've played this so cool. Talked about Jake. About how my family doesn't know the meaning of *scared*, ha-ha. All "I'll do everybody proud."

"Are you okay?"

"I'm fine. Sorry. I think I'm just nervous."

More pacing as I try to play it off. A "nothing to see here" smile in full effect. I can't get off the rock quick enough.

"Hey, *hey*." She stands up and looks into my eyes. "What did I say?"

"Nothing," I say. "Really. I'm just tired. You know?"

Can she still tell when I'm lying, see through me as easily as she could when we were kids? Not even the smallest lie was safe then, and I hated it. She stares at me with the same knowing look now, an unblinking focus intent on figuring out exactly what's happening inside my head.

"We should probably go back down," I say. "It sounds like everybody's getting pretty animated."

"Yeah, sure." She starts to say something but swallows it. I take a couple of quick breaths and pick my way through the shadows and branches along the narrow trail until I'm standing next to the fire again, its heat oppressive against my skin.

"Where'd you two go?" Sinclair asks, grinning like a fool.

"We were talking," I say quickly. There's something in my voice, a strident panic that only gets my heart beating faster. Mallory kicks a small rock over the edge of the quarry, ignoring the entire exchange.

One of the guys in the group, Steve, whose claim to fame is that he once streaked during a football game, cocks his head to the side and says, "You and Will broke up?"

This time the confidence she uses to explain Will's absence is gone. "He's at home."

"I figured you two would be together tonight, that's all." Steve cuts his eyes to me, and I suddenly remember how else I know Steve Chapman. He sat with Will in the one class we had together, right in front of me. I don't know if they're close friends, but the way he's glaring at me seems proof enough.

"I'm doing my own thing tonight with an old friend," Mallory says, staring daggers at Steve.

"Okay, okay," he says. "Turn it down a few. I'm just asking questions."

Mallory sighs and pulls a bottle from the cooler.

"Can somebody please open this for me?"

Sinclair pulls out his lighter and pops the cap off in one quick motion, handing the bottle to Mallory.

"Look at Sinclair," Wayne says. "Dude's a Swiss army knife."

A few people laugh, and the spotlight fades off Mallory as Sinclair shows them the trick. Mallory seems normal enough, laughing when the conversation dictates and playing the part of the happy graduate. But I can tell she's faking something because I've been playing that same part for months.

Hell, I'm playing it now, sitting next to Wayne and nodding as people talk about cars they got for graduation, scholarships others shouldn't have won. On the outskirts of the group I catch Steve staring at me like he's checking up on a younger brother. When his phone rings and he stands up, cupping his hand over his ear so he can hear, Mallory walks over to me.

"We should probably go," she says, only to me.

"All right. Whenever you want to leave."

"Right now."

She tries to jump over the log I'm sitting on, accidentally kicking a beer bottle into the fire. Wayne gives a good-natured yell, but Mallory ignores him, again saying that we really need to go. But it's become impossible for me to leave anywhere lately without getting a couple of hugs and more than a few hand slaps. Mallory stands impatiently to the side as it happens.

When the last person says good-bye, she nearly drags me away from the fire.

"All right, everybody," Mallory yells over her shoulder. "Time for the Mallory show to go back on the road."

I grab her arm before she can get in the truck. When she turns around, she looks ready to get in the driver's seat and take her chances jumping the lip of the quarry.

"Steve called Will, right?" I ask.

"Yeah," she says. "And Will's probably on his way up to the quarry now. I really don't want to deal with all of that, so can we please leave?"

On cue, Steve rushes out of the darkness, putting his phone in his pocket. "Where the hell are you guys going?"

It's the way he says it. Like he wants me to knock him out.

"Go back to the party," I say. "Seriously. This isn't what you think it is."

"I know you talked to him," Mallory says, giving him a slanted look. It seems to spook Steve, who takes a step back.

"Yeah. So?"

"It's none of his business what I'm doing tonight," she says.

"Well, from what I just heard, Will might disagree with that."

They stand there, dogs readying to fight. Then Mallory smiles and goes for the throat. "You're a pretty good friend for a guy Will hasn't talked about in two years."

Steve takes another step back, as if her words were fists. But then he smiles, collecting himself. "Hey, I'm not the one who's whoring around with some asshole I just met."

And then for extra measure he says, "Slut."

I go for him, but Mallory gets in front of me, yelling my name.

"No, let him go," Steve says. "Let's see which one of you is the bigger bitch."

"Thomas, please. Let's go."

As she's saying it, Wayne and the rest of the group gather in a half circle around us. Mallory says my name one more time, soft but insistent. Then: "Don't."

When I back down, Steve says, "I always knew you were a coward."

Mallory whips around. "Would you please shut up?"

"I'm trying to help my friend," Steve says. "But maybe I'll call him back and tell him exactly what kind of a person he plans on—"

Mallory's hand is a blur across Steve's face. "Shut up," she says, her voice quiet.

That's enough for me. I take Steve by the shirt, the way you would a toddler who's about to run into the road, and drag him back to the fire with everybody following. I push him away, ready for him to come right back at me. Instead, he straightens out his shirt and cusses a guy who comes over to help.

Wayne comes up beside me, looking more than happy to get involved. But I don't need him.

"Stay away from her," I tell Steve.

"Yeah? And what are you going to do if I don't?"

"Hey, Steve," Wayne says. "You might need a pad of paper so you can jot down all the things my boy could do to you."

This punctures the tension, and a few people laugh. Not Steve.

"I'd like to see him try," he says.

Wayne is standing next to Steve now. He puts his hands on his shoulder and says, "Now, why are you going to go and ruin everybody's graduation by getting yourself killed? Sin, get this man a beer."

Sinclair grabs a beer and hands it to Steve, who, after

a second of hard staring at me, takes the bottle and says, "Whatever. Fuck him."

Wayne claps. "That's right, son. Live to fight another day."

When I turn back to my truck, Wayne steps across the fire and walks with me. "What the hell was that about?"

"Nothing. Just Steve being an asshole," I say.

Mallory is leaning against my truck, staring down at her cell phone. The screen lights up her face. "If Will comes up here, tell him we went to South Carolina or something."

"Myrtle Beach. Hell, yes. If you weren't leaving for the damned army, we'd be doing that shit right now."

"I'm going to take Mallory home," I say. "And then—"

Wayne gives me a salute, then laughs. He pulls me into a hug. "Shit, Bennett. Next time I see you you'll be one of those sexy ass men in uniform types. Hell, *that's* when we should go to Myrtle Beach."

Mallory's phone goes off, and she silences it. It rings again almost immediately.

"Be good," Wayne says. "All right?"

One more hug, and Wayne's gone, back to the fire. The last thing I hear him say is "I thought graduation was supposed to be drama free. Somebody—Sin!—beer me."

Mallory is deleting texts off her phone, then voice messages, shaking her head the whole time. Without looking up she says, "I shouldn't have slapped him. But he deserved it."

"The way I see it, you're two for two tonight," I say. "Two assholes, two more-than-appropriate hits."

She finally looks up from her phone and says, "Will's not an asshole. It's . . . complicated."

She closes her eyes, the phone buzzing in her hands. I take it from her—Will, of course—and silence it. She looks up at me, and I try to explain what I'm feeling.

"Do you remember when my dad made me cut my hair?" I ask.

She looks confused at first, but then she smiles. "You worked so hard growing it out, too. It really did look nice."

"Well, he'd argue that point with you—probably even today," I say, trying not to get distracted. "I came to school the next day, and what did you tell me?"

She laughs out loud. "That I was going to shave my head, too. I was nothing if not loyal."

"Wait. *What?*"

"I was going to shave my head," Mallory says flatly.

"I don't remember that!"

Mallory screws up her face momentarily and says,

"You don't? We had that whole conversation about how scary I'd look." As she says it, she cups the front of her hair and pulls it behind her hand, making it look like she's bald. I laugh.

"God, I don't remember any of this. But that's not the point. What I remember is—" Her phone goes off in my hand, and I want to do something dramatic, throw it into the dark quarry. Instead, I silence it and put it in my pocket.

"I've got an idea."

CHAPTER EIGHT

The playground is older but otherwise no different from when we were in elementary school. Mallory climbs the steps to the clock tower, which seemed impossibly tall to us as first graders and the height of freedom when we were in fifth grade. She runs her hand along the smooth wood, recently repainted. White as cotton. If I wanted to, I could jump and touch her hand.

"I always loved it here," she says, surveying the playground. "Do you remember when I told everyone the wood had termites so nobody else would play on this thing?"

"That worked for about five minutes."

"I still hate Miss Hoffman for ruining that scam."

"We were prodigies, obviously."

She finally smiles. "Something like that."

I stand on the bottom of the slide, coming eye level with Mallory. "But it's finally worked out," I say. "The whole place, all to ourselves."

She rolls her eyes. "C'mon, I want to swing."

I pull myself up, over the railing and follow her across the suspension bridge, still able to hold both of us, and down a second slide that's barely wide enough for me. And then she's sitting on the swings again, just like I remember. She could have scabbed knees and a fist in my face the way she's hanging on to the swing's chains, leaning forward as she talks.

"Five bucks says you quit before me."

I look at the swing and think about the 120 pounds that have come to pass since I've last been on it. But Mallory doesn't wait; she pumps her arms and legs, sweeping back and forth in front of me. I jump on my swing and try to catch up.

The wind mutes her laughter, the shriek of objection when she realizes I'm going higher than she does. She tries to change physics, but the extra work she's doing only slows her down. Soon we're moving together. Our feet almost touch heaven, and then we come back, falling just as quickly as we rose. Over and over again we rise and fall, making eye contact each time our backs are at the sky. On the next push forward, at the height of the swing, Mallory lets go.

When she lands, I'm sure she's broken something. The notebook, which has been in her pocket, ends up a few feet away. Her body convulses on the ground, and I leap off my swing after her. But once I kneel down next to her, I realize she's laughing.

"Did you see that? I never got this far as a kid."

"You almost hit the monkey bars."

"Exactly. Third graders ain't got nothing on me." She struggles to catch her breath before saying, "Life was better when we were kids, wasn't it? Do you remember how long it took for Christmas? For our birthdays? A year took *forever.* You had to figure out all kinds of things to do while you waited. Now it's just like"— she makes a zipper noise and swipes a finger through the air—"zoom. Done. You make a decision, and it happens. You barely have to wait for anything."

"I don't know. Look at Sinclair. He's going to be waiting for NASCAR for a long time."

I realize too late that when she laughs this time, it's different. It turns to tears, which quickly turn to all-out sobbing. She grabs my neck and holds tight. I can feel her tears on my shirt.

"It's stupid," she says. "I was so stupid."

"It's going to be okay. You can call him. Right now, if you want."

This makes her cry harder, and when she shakes her head, I'm confused. Before, I would've thought it was your typical graduation breakup. Or maybe it was just a fight that got out of hand. But Steve was so adamant, such an asshole . . . it doesn't make sense.

A phone vibrates, and Mallory touches her pockets until we both realize it's mine. She lets go of me and wipes her eyes, as I look at the screen: Mom. I silence the phone, and it's not dark two seconds before it lights up again, buzzing angrily in my hands.

"You should answer it," she says.

"They just want me to come home," I say.

She's quiet for a second. "Maybe we should. You've got so much going on. You don't need all of this."

The truth of her statement feels true, a blanket securely wrapped around me. But she still looks so lost, enough

that I have no idea how I could even begin to help her—
even if we stayed out all night and a hundred more after
that. Whenever I got this way, her answers seemed effort-
less. Her plans, perfect. And now that it's finally my turn,
I'm coming up short.

"Well, we need to go bury the can before we go home,"
I say.

It's all I've got. Every card, on the table.

She sniffs, nods. "And the sign, too. That way it's
always there. Our little secret."

I want to take her by the hand, put my arm around her,
something. But when she stands up and wipes her legs off,
it feels like an ending, a natural stopping point. Something
neither of us can deny. As we walk to my truck in silence,
that same hollowness that's filled my stomach for months
returns. All that's left is to go home, take my lumps, and
then wake up in the morning and finally leave.

CHAPTER NINE

When we get to the bridge, I park the truck in the same place as before. Mallory opens her door, carrying the coffee can and sign with equal reverence. We bury the can in its original hole first and then wrap the sign in an old T-shirt and start digging a bigger, wider hole together.

Mallory is quiet, but the work unearths something inside me, kinks in my memories of these sorts of moments. They always had an old-movie nostalgia to them, a fuzzy warmth. But more often than not, when we found ourselves here at the end of the day, it was always just like this: wringing out one more hour before I had to go catch hell for whatever reason.

The hole's plenty deep, but I'm still digging. Still trying to figure out why my dad has always pushed Jake and, in a different way, me. I see so many people at school who have succeeded in sports or academics, who are tough and brave, and they don't have to worry about this shit. The expectations they carry begin and end with personal happiness.

Mallory reaches out and touches my arm. I'm dirty, out of breath, and on the verge of tears. She picks up the sign, holding it high for both of us to see one last time, and gently puts it in the oversized hole. It only takes a few seconds to cover it back up. Like we were never here.

"We need a rock to mark it. Unless you want to make a treasure map," she says. "Sixteen steps north. When you see the hooked nose rock, turn left and stand on one foot. That sort of thing."

I don't say anything, and she bumps me once with her hip.

"I don't think anybody's going to come looking for it," I say.

"No, for when *we* come back," she says. "Next time."

I have to look away, staring into the dark field as she

searches for a rock. We didn't come out here much at night. Fourth of July, the rare times when our parents left us alone with Jake as a baby-sitter. Even then we had to be sneaky. We had to move quickly and deliberately. Half the time the sneaking out was the best part.

That's how it comes to me.

Mallory's putting a large river rock—I have no idea how it got down here—on top of the recently overturned dirt. When she sees me, I must look insane because a flash of panic comes across her face quicker than I can get the word out.

"*Snap!*"

Mallory's face transforms, her eyes wide and alive. "I know you just didn't drop Snap! on me right now, Bennett. Jesus. Snap!"

The game isn't complicated. Run into the darkness and hide. Whoever can sneak up on the other one first and whisper, "Snap!" wins. The beauty of the game is that you can play with an entire neighborhood or just two or three. A lot of kids wanted to get Snapped! early so they could go back and sit on the porch with their friends. But forget that noise. Winning Snap! was better than money back then. Of course we played in the neighborhoods; who didn't? But the field was ours, and we never invited anyone out here to play with us.

"We should play Snap!" I say, looking out into the dark field. Like a broken ankle waiting to happen.

Still.

This is the card I can play for her. For both of us.

"I don't know," Mallory says. "Your parents are going to be pissed at me."

"One round, and then I'll take you home," I say. "It shouldn't take long, seeing as I'm undefeated."

"Okay, slow down. You may need to look up the definition of *undefeated*."

I feign surprise, offense. "I seem to remember you refusing to play and running home. Multiple times."

Her face twists into actual shock. "Are you kidding? That was *you*."

"No way. I never did that." But then it comes back to me, and I pause just long enough that Mallory starts nodding enthusiastically.

"Yeah, you know. Own your shame."

"Well, before that I was definitely undefeated."

"I feel like you've been doing a lot of drugs since we last hung out," she says. "Even in the most backward of memories, how does that happen?"

She's laughing, looking out into the field, likely already planning a strategy. Despite my talk, Mallory was preternatural in her abilities. She makes no sound, and her body seems to fold into the shadows. I want to play so badly. I want to win.

She sighs. "Fine. If we're going to do this, we need to stretch first. We're old now, and safety needs to come first."

She makes a show of touching her toes. As soon as I bend over, she laughs. Then she screams, "Go!" and takes off running into the darkness, laughing as she disappears.

I move quickly, but carefully. Mallory always liked hiding just outside my vision, whispering "Snap!" when I passed and ending the game minutes after it began. But I can't see anything now, so I move toward the road, away from Mallory's initial line.

I know exactly where I'm going, but I still move carefully through the darkness. There are two strategies in Snap! The first is to move, to glide across the play area like a shadow, snapping every person you come across. The second—the patient player's tactic—is to find a spot, hunker down, and pick people off as they come by. And that's what I plan to do: wait until she gets frustrated and starts hunting.

My eyes slowly adjust to the night, and I begin to see Mallory everywhere. A bush looks like her hair on my right, and I swear her elbow is showing behind a tree twenty feet in front of me. But Snap! turns every branch breaking, every chirping insect into Mallory about to attack. I crouch down, looking across the field. Nothing is moving, so I go—probably too fast.

I don't see the dip in the grass and nearly fall right into it. I stagger into a crouch, breathing hard and scanning the field for any sign of Mallory. My entire body shakes with anticipation as I try not to move.

When I was a kid, I'd hide behind trees and jump over streams. Running from, toward, invisible enemies, the kind my dad always talked about. I never thought about dying or how it would feel to be pinned down as bullets cut the air above me. Lately I haven't been able to think about anything else. And as I crouch here, watching an ant crawl across a blade of grass, I work to slow my breathing.

Footsteps like cannon fire come across the quiet field, and everything else disappears. To my right, a shadow moves, matching the footsteps. She sounds like a bull moving through the field, which surprises me enough that I almost stand up and ask her if everything's okay. Instead, I wait until she's standing ten feet in front of me and whisper, "Snap!"

Will turns around and yells. I do, too, which makes me wonder where Mallory is—if she'll come running.

"What the hell are you doing?" Will asks. And then, almost immediately: "Where's Mallory?"

"Me? What are *you* doing out here?"

"Where's Mallory?"

I scan the field as casually as I can. "She's not here."

"But you know where she is."

"Man, c'mon. I dropped her off at her house and haven't seen her since."

Will studies me, but the lies now fall easily from my mouth. He looks angry and hurt. "I know you were up at the quarry," he says.

I try to make my voice even. "We went up there with Wayne and Sinclair. We talked about you, actually. And then your friend Steve started acting like an asshole."

Will nods, looks around the field. "Well, that seems about right."

"If you want my opinion, give her some space. For

tonight at least." He starts to object, but I talk over him. "You can't keep calling her. I mean, you know what she's like."

He sighs and says, "She's making me crazy. All I want to do is talk to her."

"So you thought you'd come search for her in an empty field?"

He looks confused. "What?"

"You're in the middle of a field at midnight."

He thinks about this for a second and says, "So are you."

I hesitate, long enough to make it seem like I don't know why I'm lying down in a field in the middle of the night. I go with the old standby.

"I'm leaving for the army in the morning and wanted to be alone."

He eyes me and says, "I get that. Still, it's kind of weird."

Something moves in the distance, and my entire body becomes a knot. I suddenly have visions of Mallory walking up, having it out with Will right in front of me. I don't know if I want them to make up or not—at least right now. Because then it really would be over.

I say, "So . . . why are you out here?"

Will reaches toward his back pocket. "I lost my wallet when the car got stuck. I just realized."

He pauses, and I look at the ground, feeling bad for a moment. I kick at a rock and say, "Yeah, sorry. I didn't think you guys would be stupid enough to follow me into the field."

"Jeremy is pissed. They had to tow the car out."

I can't help it; I laugh. So does Will.

"I don't know what he was thinking." And then something switches on his face, like he realizes we shouldn't be having such a casual conversation. "If you point me in the right direction, I'll see if I can find it. You can get back to your, uh, alone time."

I'm trying to mask my indecision: let him wander around by himself or go with him. Neither option is ideal, but I'm pretty sure I can't convince him to leave without his wallet. So I tell him I'll help him search for it, and he agrees after a moment of apprehension.

It takes only a few minutes before I see where the car entered the mud, as well as the wide swath carved when it was pulled out. As we walk up, I am struck by how perfect a place this would be to hide in a game of Snap! And then I'm worried because maybe Mallory is here, hidden in the mud like a B movie commando. But as we pick our way through, both of us with our eyes down, her hand doesn't come shooting up from the ground to grab our ankles. Still, I half expect to hear her voice in my ear, to win the game without Will's ever knowing she was here.

"It could be anywhere," Will says, bending over to squint at the ground for a moment before standing up. "Perfect. Exactly how this night should end."

I walk softly, trying not to step on his wallet, at the same time making as much noise as possible just in case Mallory hasn't figured out what's happening yet. Saying his name whenever I address him and as loudly as I can without seeming even more weird. Every few seconds Will lets loose a shallow exhale. I can't help myself.

"What happened between you two?" He sighs again, this time long and emphatic. Even in the limited light he looks scattered. "I don't know. I thought everything was great. If she'd pick up the phone and listen to me, I'm sure we could figure it out."

He pulls out his phone and gets ready to dial. I jump toward him and say, "Hey, good idea. Use that to find your wallet."

I reach in my pocket and power down Mallory's phone

at the same time. Too close. I walk over to him and say, "On second thought, you should probably do this in the morning. When you can see."

"I need my wallet," he says, and it doesn't look like he's in any hurry to leave. He walks slowly, bending over to check the ground like he's on the beach hunting for shells. I try to tell him I need to go home and pack. When that doesn't work, I take a shot and say he's probably making it worse by walking around.

"You could step on it and grind it in. You'd never find it," I say, hoping my logic penetrates his melancholy. Behind him, I think I see a shadow moving across the grass. When I look again, it's gone.

He nods but doesn't move. Instead, he stares at me for a long time, finally saying, "You'd tell me if she was here, right?"

"Yeah." I'm unsure if the sick feeling in my gut is from the lie or the truth of her proximity. But he nods again and hesitates before offering his hand to me.

"Good luck." He says it sheepishly, like I haven't heard it before. Still, I shake his hand.

"She used to talk about you," he says. "Not a lot, but every so often. She missed you, I think. Maybe you could give her a call when you get back. She'd like that."

Then he turns around and walks away. As he disappears into the night, I'm not sure if I've won something or not.

I tear through the field once he's gone. I check the ditch by the road, the tall grass near the tree line, but she isn't in any of her old spots. When at last I come back to the bridge, she's sitting on the tailgate of my truck, staring out into the field.

"Hey," I say, out of breath, "Will was here."

"I saw." I expected anger, but her voice is soft. "Is he gone?"

"Uh, yeah. He was looking for his wallet."

"What did you guys talk about?"

"What else? World politics," I say. When it doesn't get a laugh, I add, "I had the best hiding spot ever, and he pretty much ruined it because he walked across the field and I thought it was you, so I Snapped! him. Let's just say we were both surprised to see each other."

She smiles this time, rubbing her eyes.

"So he thinks you're out here playing Snap! by yourself. That's . . . wonderful."

"I told him I wanted to be alone. In a field. In the middle of the night."

This cracks me up.

"It happens," she says, and this gets her laughing, too. "God, tonight is so messed up. I'm sorry about this."

"What else do I have to do? Join the army?"

This time, though, she shuts down, staring at me the way Will did, a kind of hurting disbelief in her eyes. And for a moment we're both quiet, looking at each other, waiting for the other one to say something that will give the conversation momentum again.

Mallory shakes her head, like she's trying to forget a bad dream, and says, "Do you ever worry that you're going to miss out on something by leaving? Like, obviously the army's a good decision—something you want to do. But do you ever wish maybe you had decided to go to college?"

"I don't know if I could get into college," I say.

"Even community college. Just anything other than what people expect."

A familiar tightness pulls at my lungs. If there was a time to tell anyone, this is it. It would be so easy—open my mouth and say the words.

I'm not going to the army.

"I went and visited my sister down at Chapel Hill last year," she says. "And I know it sounds stupid, but that weekend was kind of a revelation. I didn't want to come back."

Tell her. Right now. Tell her everything.

"But I know Will wouldn't be able to get in; he's already got a job working at his dad's church as the youth pastor. He might go to Bible college or something, but right now this is it for him. But sometimes I want to go away, pick up and leave. I can't explain it."

She stops talking, kicking her heel against the tire of my truck until she looks up and says, "Do you think that makes me a bad person?"

I think about what to say for a long time. "Sometimes you need to do what's best for you, even if it's going to make people upset."

She doesn't agree or disagree with me, just kicks the tire until I swear her heel makes a dent in the rubber. I watch her, wondering if she really would leave, if she could cut her ties as easily as I'm about to cut mine. And for a second I imagine us with the sun at our backs, leaving North Carolina together.

"Well, I'm going to let myself believe that—at least for tonight," she says. "So where was it?"

"What?" I ask.

"Your spot. Where were you hiding?"

"Oh. Well, I'm not sure I want to tell you, because it's pretty much a guaranteed win if we ever decide to do this again."

She looks bored, almost offended. "The hollow tree."

"I'm not telling you."

"The tires?"

"Seriously, it's not going to happen."

"You are a man of limited options, Thomas. I'm going to figure it out eventually."

"*Limited options*? Jesus, that's the worst thing anybody's ever said to me."

She's smiling as she says, "If you don't tell me, I swear I'll never play this game with you ever again."

It's childish and stupid, and it totally works.

"Fine. There's this dip in the middle of the field—"

"Oh." She turns away unimpressed.

"Hey, what does that mean?"

"Nothing, I just thought you had something good."

"It's perfect," I say.

"It's in the middle of the field, not to mention completely indefensible. I could get at you from any direction.

What happens if I came up behind you?"

"I'd hear you." She stares at me until I say, "It's still a good spot. You can't see me until you're right on top of the dip."

"And you can't see out of it! Seriously, I'm getting worried about your chances as a soldier."

For the first time I don't feel a shock of panic or relief when somebody mentions being a soldier. Instead, I explain how I almost fell in.

"So you wouldn't have time for a sneak attack because you wouldn't know it was there," I say.

She counters this and every other argument I make until the effect of Will's appearance has disappeared, if only temporarily. She holds up her hand.

"Stop. Please." She shakes her head in disbelief. "If you're not going to listen to reason, then—"

Her smile is slanted to one side as she leans forward. And damn it, I know what she's going to do a second too late. A second before she leans close to my face and says: "Snap! I win."

CHAPTER TEN

Neither of us moves when my phone goes off in my pocket, not the first or second time. Mom can wait. Tonight's finally over, and we both know it. I keep hoping Mallory will break the silence, but she sits next to me, equally content and quiet, and I decide to take it for as long as I can.

Tomorrow—or today, I guess—is finally here, and I'm only hours away from going. Where? For how long? I have no idea. Up until this point there was no need for planning. I had some money, and I could camp and eat on the cheap. Isn't that how people start new lives? First they get up the gumption to leave, and then they do it. Let the chips fall where they may, that sort of thing.

I can get a job working at a gas station or in fast food. Make enough money to last until August or however long it takes for Dad to cool down. Christmas at the latest. There's no way Mom would let me miss the holidays.

Mallory jumps off the gate so quickly I'm sure something's bitten her. She pats at her pockets like her clothes are on fire.

"Oh, God. Oh, God." She looks at her hands and then goes back to searching her pockets. "No, no, no."

"What's wrong? What's happening?"

"I'm so *stupid*."

I hop off the gate and grab her by the shoulders. Her face worries me.

"I lost the ring. I took it off, and now it's gone."

"The ring," I say.

I saw it just after Christmas, when she was checking out a book at the library. Her friends were standing around, cooing and carrying on. When she saw me looking, I could tell she was embarrassed, hiding her hand behind a book she was holding. It was small, the sort of thing you bought at a kiosk in the mall. A ruby maybe. But most likely red glass, cut and shaped to look better than it was. For the next few weeks I'd catch snippets of conversations, girls fawning over Will, maybe the only guy in high school with enough balls to buy a girl a ring.

She crumples over and then drops into a squat, panicking. "I only took it off because I was pissed at him, but it was in my pocket. I put it in my pocket when I came to your house."

"Maybe it's in the truck," I say, going to the passenger side. I search the floorboards, the seats, even the glove compartment. Then, because she hasn't moved, I search the driver's side. When I still don't find it, I pull out my phone—nine unread texts from Mom—and use it to check under the seats. Nothing.

"I need to find it," she says, standing up suddenly. Her face is absent, like Jake's. Void of possibility, of any hope to find resolution. For a second it scares me; how helpless I feel. It's a ring in a field at midnight.

I turn around and walk slowly, searching for any gleam of light in the dirt.

"Maybe you lost it when you were hiding," I say, beginning to feel the panic, too. If anything, Mallory is growing calmer by the second, but I'm not. "Where were you?"

"The tree line," she says. And for a second I'm annoyed. I wouldn't have ever found her because that's always been out of bounds. I wish I could mention it, could see the indignation—maybe it would be guilt—flash across her face seconds before she gave me the definitive explanation as to why I'm wrong.

Instead, I point my cell phone to the ground as we walk, searching for a ring that is likely invisible. Part of me doesn't want her to find it, which I realize is childish and petty. Then I imagine finding the ring, holding it up. Seeing the relief overtake her face, transforming her back into who she really is.

When we get to the tree line, she points at a large stump, once an even larger tree. "I was sitting there, waiting for you."

We both drop to our knees, searching through the piles of dead grass, the leaves. We're not halfway around the stump when she sits on top of it and says, "This is pointless. I probably lost it when we were at the park. Or the quarry. Or the hotel. For all I know, some guy at the campfire just gave it to his girlfriend."

She hugs her knees, and I have no idea what to say. Part of me wants to be like, It's just a stupid ring. But then I think about Jake and remember that sometimes even the littlest things will send him spinning. Seeing a kid walking a dog. A man jogging. Nobody knows the dread of seeing him fade away.

"It's going to be okay," I say. "He'll understand."

She laughs, which surprises and encourages me until I see her face.

"No, he won't. Trust me."

"When I talked to him in the field, he seemed like he'd do anything to make things right."

"Well, this is different," she says softly.

All I can do is mechanically pat her shoulder and offer up more and more general assurances. I hate not knowing how to fix this, so I stand up and pull out my cell phone again. I walk around the stump, hoping I'll see a flash.

"Thomas, stop. Sit down."

"We might have missed it," I say.

"Really, you don't have to do this. And you're right, it's a ring. He'll get over it. Please just sit with me."

I sit next to her on the stump, easily big enough for both of us. It reminds me of just how enormous the tree used to be, a hickory. We spent an entire summer nailing salvaged pieces of wood to its trunk, creating a makeshift ladder that unlocked the tallest branches, which we climbed, higher and higher until they began bowing dangerously underneath us. You could see downtown, our houses—to the next state, we liked to believe. It got hit by lightning and ended up getting cut down sometime during our sophomore year. It's weird to think of something so big disappearing overnight. But even dead, it sticks to the earth like a monument, too stubborn to be completely erased.

When my phone buzzes again, Mallory reaches for her pocket and panics. "Oh, God, my phone." She looks frantic before I pull it out of my pocket. She takes it, notices it's turned off, and says, "Did you do this?"

"Will was trying to call you when I was talking to him. I thought that might be awkward."

"Thanks," she says.

"We could go buy a ring. In the morning."

She pauses and then says, "It was his grandmother's."

It's like the roots of the stump reach up and tie me to the ground. Somehow knowing that he didn't pick the ring up on a whim makes me want to find it more, and I don't understand why.

"He gave it to me for Christmas. Know what I got him?" There's an awful weight in her eyes as she says it. "A certificate to play paintball."

"Sounds pretty good to me."

"Yeah, but not when somebody gives you a family heirloom. I mean, what a moron, right? Who does that?" She exhales and says, "Anyway, then I put it on and—"

She stops, won't look at me.

"What?"

"It's stupid. You'll think I'm an idiot."

"I already think you're an idiot."

She exhales again, louder and more forceful. Keeps kicking her foot against the base of the stump.

"I felt connected to somebody again." She stares up at me, her eyes like two hands pushing into my chest. "It had been a long time since I felt that way about someone."

It's how I expect it might feel to fall through a trapdoor, to have solid ground underneath your feet and then, suddenly, there's nothing. Falling and falling into the black. I put my arm around her. She has small shoulders, thin and fragile like a bird's wing.

"I'm sorry," I say.

Because she lost the ring and because we lost so much time. Because I've been such an ignorant prick and because right now I have no idea what else to do or say. She looks up at me, blinking as a piece of hair falls into her eyes. Those eyes haven't changed since we were kids, big and blue and incapable of hiding what she's really feeling.

And then I kiss her.

I want it to be electric, to have some romantic music swell around us as we realize this is the point of everything. But it's a mistake. And I know it immediately. She pulls away from me, and the panic in her eyes mirrors exactly what's happening inside me.

Sirens wailing. A chorus of "Oh, Shit! Oh, Shit! Oh, Shit!" But I can't move my mouth, can't apologize or explain why I thought it was a good idea.

I'm going to be sick.

"What was that?" She stands up.

"Mallory, I'm sorry. I don't know why I did that—" My phone goes off, and I don't want to look at it—I already know who it is—but Mallory turns away from me, and it keeps buzzing in my hands, so I answer it with a yell.

"Jesus, what!"

"Thomas?"

I can hear Jake breathing on the other line, like he's been jogging. He used to run everywhere; people always talked about it. He could go for days. Now it sounds like a rattling engine ready to die.

"Jake. What do you need?" I have no idea how to make

my voice sound normal with him on the phone. "Why are you calling me?"

"Do you realize how fucking stupid you're being right now?"

"Tell Dad I'll be home soon."

"I'm not at home," he says, as if he can't believe I'd make that assumption. The heavy breathing, the background noise: it sounds like he's in the middle of the interstate.

"Where are you?"

"At the bridge."

"What bridge?"

"River Road. I want you to meet me here."

There was a time when this call would've been everything. Jake wanting me to meet him anywhere. Now my entire body fills with panic, erasing any embarrassment I feel about what happened with Mallory. She fades away as I talk slowly.

"What are you doing at the bridge?"

He curses, spits, and then says, "I just need to talk to you before you leave."

"Are you okay?"

He pauses, only a second or two, but it feels like my entire life is passing by. Then he says, "Can you be here soon? We need to do this now."

I want to know what, why, but the longer I stay on the phone, the longer he'll be out there waiting.

"Yeah, fine. I need to drop off Mallory first. But I'll be there."

He doesn't say anything, just hangs up—there one minute and gone the next.

I hold the phone in my hand, unsure of where to start with Mallory. "I need to go," I say. "Jake's out on River Road, at the bridge."

She doesn't move, doesn't speak.

"I can drop you off before I go."

Still nothing. I take a step toward her, expecting she'll just follow me wordlessly to the truck. We'll share an awkward ride back to her house, and I'll live with the guilt of ruining this once again for—how long? Months? Years? However long, I have the undeniable sense that I've finally ended everything between us.

But the anxiety about Jake climbs up my neck and breathes in my ear, trumping everything else.

"Either way, I need to go."

She spins around and faces me. "You can't do that again," she says. "Promise me you aren't going to do that again."

"I'm sorry."

"Don't be sorry; just promise you're not going to do that again. I have a boyfriend, and it's bad enough that I lost the ring, that I'm out with you instead of him. Plus, *that* isn't what tonight is about. It's not what *we're* about, Thomas. So you have to promise me right now that you're never going to do that again."

"I know, Mallory. I promise. And I am sorry."

She still looks a little angry when she says, "And I'm not going home. So stop being stupid."

"I don't know if you should come," I say carefully. I've already told her about Jake, but seeing him, having him focus on her with those empty eyes, is another story.

"Well, I don't care what you want right now, so shut up about it already. What I want is to go to River Road to see why in the hell your brother feels the need to further screw up my graduation night with all his crazy."

It stings, and she sees how I flinch immediately.

"Now I'm sorry," she says quietly. And then we stand there, unable to deny how weird it's become. But I don't have time for awkwardness, not now.

CHAPTER ELEVEN

River Road is long, cutting across four counties and eventually getting swallowed by Highway 10 before they both spill into the interstate. The bridge, an old metal structure that crosses the river, soon to be the Specialist Jake Bennett Bridge, sits exactly in the middle of the county. I've known this place since birth, but every turn feels like a surprise as I try to get to Jake.

"Any idea what he wants?" Mallory says, her voice still noticeably tentative. "Does he go out to the bridge a lot? That's a pretty long walk from your house."

She rubs her wrist as she talks, both feet on the dashboard. Trying so hard to be casual. The truth is, I have no idea what Jake does when I'm not around. This phone call was the most animated he's been in months. If he's not watching a movie or eating, he's in a mobile catatonic state. Moving only enough to remind you that he still exists.

I fantasize about miracles, that he's been magically healed in the past two hours. That we'll arrive at the bridge and he'll be there, grinning like he did in his yearbook pictures. The guy jokingly voted Most Likely to Be Arrested. The football star. He never seemed to stop smiling, even when everybody else was worried about college or SAT scores. Jake was mythic to everyone.

The bridge comes into view first, then Jake. He sidearms a rock, and it skips across the water as I park the truck. The backpack sits open at his feet.

Dad never liked to fish but wanted us around the water as kids. So we'd get in the truck and drive to the river on weekends. He'd send us out to find the perfect stones, flat and smooth, and we'd throw them until our arms ached and the sun died behind us. We'd go to Mountain View Barbeque and have hamburgers, fries, milk shakes, never returning before dark. Half the time Dad would catch hell because Mom had dinner on the table and we were already busting at the seams.

When Mallory and I get out of the truck, Jake zips up the backpack and puts it on his shoulder.

"Thanks for coming," he says.

"Yeah. Of course."

Jake and I never had the kind of relationship where I'd go into his room and tell him about girls or what was going on in my life. Dad was never the sort to share his feelings, and he didn't want us doing it either. I didn't understand it, but it never really mattered, I guess. It wasn't until I was over at a friend's house and saw the way they were with each other that I knew we were different. In another world, maybe I'd come to this bridge all red faced and embarrassed and confess to Jake how I stupidly kissed my best friend.

"Good to see you again, Jake," Mallory says from behind me. Jake nods at the dark water, otherwise motionless. I don't know what he wants or if he'll even talk with Mallory around, so I motion her back to the truck. Mallory hesitates, then walks away. When she's leaning against the truck, I turn to Jake, but he is still facing the river.

"Is Mom freaking out?" I ask.

"Mom's always freaking out," he says.

"True," I admit. I try to read his face, his body. Searching for any indication that he might do something dangerous to himself. He's had the same pair of pants on for three days, and Dad has been itching to tell him to shave for longer than that. His gray army T-shirt is covered in stains and hangs from his shoulders. More than anything, he seems smaller. Not in size. Just in everything else. He sets the backpack on the ground again and scratches his face, his other hand still cupping the rocks.

I stare back at the river for a few seconds before I say, "So why are we here?"

"I haven't gotten you ready," he says. "That's on me. And we need to change that before you go tomorrow."

"Get me ready? Jake, c'mon." I touch his shoulder, and he shakes his head, more a twitch than a denial. "I'm ready. I've done the PT. I can do one hundred push-ups now—probably more than you."

It's a weak joke, and I surprise myself by letting it fly. Of course he ignores it.

"I'm not talking about push-ups. Listen to me," he says. "Everything you do follows you. And you need to know about it before you go. Every action has a reaction. Every good or bad thing you do has a way to fix it."

It sounds like a mash-up of something he learned in

science and a greeting card. It's so bankrupt of sense, of meaning.

"I fucked up," he says. "And I need to fix it. For both of us."

He takes a step toward the bridge, and my body seizes. I reach a hand toward him. "Maybe we should go home and talk to Mom and Dad."

This would normally make him laugh, and I can't believe I'm even saying it. But I don't know what else to do. How to make him stop being so vague.

Jake reaches back and throws another rock high into the air. The moon catches it, a flash against the sky, before it drops into the water. Something goes cold inside me.

"What was that?"

He cocks his arm again, but before he can throw anything, I grab him by the shirt. There's a medal in his hand, a simple brown star dangling from a red, white, and blue ribbon.

"What the hell are you doing?"

"Let go of me."

He tries to wrestle free, and for the first time in my life I stop him. For the first time I'm stronger than he is. I put him against the railing, and the medal he was holding falls to the ground. As soon as it happens, Jakes stops struggling. He goes limp in my arms.

"Jake, what are you doing?"

"I'm doing this for you. Don't you get it? First the medals and then—" He motions to the backpack.

"Jake, man. I don't understand. *What* are you doing for me?"

He's fading in front of me, and I can't let that happen now. I want to slap him, the way Dad did to one of his army buddies who passed out on our porch one night. Right in the face.

"Where are the other medals?"

"They're gone," he says.

I look out into the river, impossibly black and who knows how deep. I let go of him and walk in circles, trying to think. Should I call Mom and Dad? Maybe they would finally take him to the hospital; maybe this will finally force them to see who Jake has become. But then I would be stuck, too. There's no way they'd let me walk out of the emergency room or psychiatric ward—wherever they put him—and go to the recruiter's office alone.

Mallory yells just as I see Jake's arm move. The last medal arcs against the sky like it has wings.

Jake doesn't move as I sprint toward the bridge, as I jump off the side and drop twenty feet into the river. I expect it to be cold. Instead, the warm water swallows me. I sink until my legs disappear into the wet mud at the bottom. Almost immediately a sharp pain travels up my right leg. When I pull up, it feels like I've lost my entire leg. But I still try to swim, to move, to catch even the smallest flicker in the dark water.

CHAPTER TWELVE

I dive down five more times before I finally listen to Mallory and get out of the river. My calf pulses blood, the cut long and deep. When Mallory sees it, her breath catches. Jake doesn't move.

"Oh, God," she says, bending over as I limp toward Jake. "What were you thinking?"

I ignore Mallory and shove Jake with both hands, nearly falling.

"What the hell?" He doesn't answer, but I keep at him. I'm pushing him, trying to force him to react, to do something, even if it means taking a punch. I want to know he's alive, even a little bit.

Only when I go for the backpack does he come to life, jumping backward and holding it away from me like it might explode. Mallory is shouting, too, trying to get my attention. When she grabs me, I reluctantly face her.

"Thomas, you need to go to the hospital."

"I'm fine," I say, turning back to Jake. I want to know why he threw the medals off the bridge. Why he can't just tell me what's wrong, what's happening inside his head. I want to know why he cares more about some damn backpack than what just happened.

She steps back in front of me and points to my leg. "You're bleeding."

I try to step around Mallory, but my leg buckles. She tries to look me in the eyes, but I'm so pissed at Jake I can't focus on anything else. "Hey, *hey*," she says. "You need stitches. And a tetanus shot. We're going to the hospital."

"What the hell is he doing?" I ask, finally looking her in the eyes. This softens her face, her words.

She turns and looks at Jake. "I don't know. But we have to take care of you first. We'll take him with us, and then . . ." Her voice trails off.

"I shouldn't even care," I say.

"Of course you should," she says. "He's your brother."

A lot of good that's done so far because I can't shake the feeling that if I had taken even the smallest of actions to help him, we wouldn't be standing here right now. But what can I do? Even the simplest moves he makes can't be anticipated. It's like living with a bomb that could go off in a hundred different ways.

Mallory looks down at my leg.

"But really, that cut. It's deep."

"I'm not leaving here without him," I say. Jake is back near the edge of the bridge, hands on the railing and chin dropped to his chest. He looks like a fighter resting in his corner between rounds.

"Wait here," she says. I object, try to follow her, but the first step I take sends a shiver of pain up my leg that nearly brings me to the ground. She walks over to Jake, puts a hand on his shoulder. I can't hear what she's saying; but he eventually nods, and Mallory walks back to me.

"Okay, let's go," she says. "I'm driving."

"Is he coming?"

"Yeah, he's coming, but I told him he has to sit in the bed because of your leg."

"Wait." I hobble after her. "What did you say to him?"

She pauses but doesn't turn around as she says, "I told him you needed him."

The hospital is only a few miles away, and the emergency room is packed with every malady one would expect after midnight. In the corner a man holds a blood-soaked rag over his left eye. A woman cradles a toddler in her arms. Two seats away from me a man dutifully presses an ice pack against his wrist, purple and bulbous. Jake stands against the far wall, naturally camouflaged with the infirm.

Mallory examines my leg from every position she can manage in the seat next to me.

"It's fine," I say.

She doesn't believe me, but that doesn't matter. My real concern is Jake. Every time he shifts against the wall, mostly trying to get a better view of the infomercial that's playing silently above him on the mounted television, I move forward in my seat like a sprinter at the starting line. Ready to chase him down the hallway, pain be damned. Mallory puts her hand on my shoulder, gently pushing me back into the chair.

"He's okay," she says. And then, as if she realizes that's

not exactly right, she adds, "He's not going anywhere. All right?"

We sit this way until a tired-looking woman in blue scrubs comes through the large double doors and calls my name. Jake keeps leaning against the wall, oblivious. I wait a second, and Mallory pointedly says his name, but nothing. When the nurse calls for me again, I raise my hand and struggle to my feet.

The pain has become biblical now that the adrenaline is gone, but I try not to let the nurse or Mallory see how much it hurts as we walk to the room. I need to get out of here and figure out what I'm going to do with Jake. However, as soon as I'm on the gurney, my head drops onto the shallow hospital pillow, and any fight I had left disappears. My body collapses.

It doesn't stop the nurse, who sticks a thermometer in my mouth and wraps a blood pressure cuff around my arm. As it expands, she watches the dial, not saying anything until the air releases.

"So what happened?"

"I cut my leg," I say. She nods, ignoring the blood that's dripping onto the paper sheet.

"And how did you do that?"

"I jumped off a bridge. Into a river."

She looks up from her notes. I open my mouth to explain, but she's already tapping something into the small laptop, shaking her head. When she finishes, she hands Mallory a large piece of gauze.

"Hold this against his leg. And try to keep him from jumping off anything else until the doctor gets here."

Mallory presses the gauze gently against my leg, and I shift my focus to the wall, trying not to worry about Jake. Generic posters of men and women with equally generic diseases stare back at me. On the opposite wall, a kitten hangs from the high branch of a tree. Any other time we would have had a field day with these.

Mallory lifts the gauze cautiously and frowns. The pain is constant, pulsing like a heartbeat in my calf. Even the smallest movement sends iron rods up my leg. When she puts the gauze back on, I wince.

"I'm sorry."

"It's just a leg," I say, trying.

"You've got two," she responds.

But it's flat, an effort where there was none before. Something is missing. Or maybe something has been added: that idiotic kiss, Jake. Now she's burdened, too.

My brother's inability to function in a spectacular way has bound us together in a new way, a connection I wish we never had to share.

A doctor comes into the room: a confident woman with a big smile and hair tied back in a ponytail. She looks at my leg and frowns.

"Please tell me jumping off bridges isn't some new graduation night challenge," she says, "because I don't want to do stitches all night."

"It's not. I was—"

"He was trying to help his brother," Mallory says, not looking at me.

"Well, that seems noble. I guess I'll give you the stitches." She smiles, taps the bed. "Okay, back in a sec."

Mallory considers my leg again once the doctor has left and says, "Real talk? That's going to be a badass scar."

"I'm going to tell people I got attacked by a puma," I say weakly.

"That's definitely sexier than saying you got it jumping off a bridge. Or at least less redneck."

I try to play. I really do. But all I can think about is getting off this table. About getting Jake in my truck and—I have no idea what. But doing something.

"I was kidding about the redneck thing," she says.

"I know. I'm sorry. I'm worried about Jake." I say. The paper sheet crinkles beneath my body as I shift my weight. "Do you mind going out there to check on him for me?"

She hesitates but then nods. "Yeah, I can do that."

"You don't have to baby-sit him or anything."

"Don't you think he's fine? I mean, I'm happy to go out there and look, but he's twenty-two years old. And your leg—I think you need somebody back here with you."

I close my eyes. I don't want to yell at Mallory or further ruin whatever we had tonight. But he could be a hundred years old, and it wouldn't matter. My leg could be in a bucket of ice on the counter, and it wouldn't matter. That's not the point. My words are sharp.

"If you want to help me, go out there and check on him. Please."

She pulls away, her eyes, her body, every word that's been spoken between us tonight. I regret the way I said it, but she saw him on the bridge, throwing his medals into the river. She has to realize that even something as simple as sitting in a waiting room is enough to warrant concern. He could walk away, could disappear in a puff of smoke. When I don't say anything else, she stands up without a word and walks out of the room.

When the doctor comes in to stitch up my leg, Mallory still isn't back. I've pissed her off, but I can't focus on whether she's mad at me or not, only on Jake. The doctor hums as she works, not saying much beyond the occasional direction to rotate my leg left or right. As the minutes pass, each one turning painfully and slow around the clock above the door, I convince myself that something's wrong. When a nurse comes into the room and I jump, the doctor tells me to keep still, that she's almost done. But I barely hear her. I have to get out of this room. I have to find Jake and Mallory.

When the doctor's finished, the same nurse comes back and tells me about pain—"nothing ibuprofen can't fix"— and then gives me the pills. I nod and nod and nod, until she hands me a piece of paper and helps me off the bed.

The first step is a killer, and I yelp. But by the time the nurse turns, ready to catch me, I'm already walking as quickly as I can manage.

I push through the heavy doors to the waiting room and don't see either Jake or Mallory. For a moment my heart stops racing, and I take a deep breath. They're outside, I tell myself. They're walking the halls. Jake is being charming, and Mallory is making it seem like she wasn't sent out to baby-sit him.

I'm halfway across the waiting room when Mallory comes rushing in. I don't need to see her face to know I was kidding myself. She opens her mouth, but I hold up my hand. I already know.

CHAPTER THIRTEEN

Mallory wants to retrace her steps—to check the cafeteria, the darkened wings of the sleeping hospital—but I limp toward the parking lot. He isn't getting a late-night snack or haunting the hallways. He's gone.

"Maybe we should wait near the emergency room," Mallory says. "Or maybe he's by the truck?"

I keep stumbling forward. He's not at the truck. He's off . . . where? Running through the shadows of our small town. But for what reason? That's the big question, of course. Why he needs to disappear. Why he can't just turn himself back on, flip whatever switch got rearranged inside his head.

When we get to the truck and he's not there, my point proved, I put my head on the hood and try to think. The pain in my leg makes it difficult to form clear thoughts, especially when Mallory's phone goes off again. I stand up, and my vision swims momentarily. I'm not sure if it's my leg or everything else.

"If you're not going to talk to him, just turn off the phone already," I say.

She silences the phone as it rings, giving me a hateful look. "This isn't my fault."

"Thanks for clearing that up," I say, tweaking my leg as I move to the driver's side of the door. I grimace, and the annoyance drifts from her face.

"Give me the keys," she says, rubbing her hand over her face. "We'll go find him."

"I don't need you to drive."

I try to take a step, and another bolt of pain shoots up my leg. She blocks the door and says, "Listen, I get that you're worried. And if you want me to help you, I will. But the first thing you need to do is stop being an asshole, and then we can start searching for him."

I'm going to scream. To punch the truck until my knuckles bleed. I have to move, to do something before all the pain and anxiety and anger that are inside me mix together and become a bomb. I halfheartedly take another step toward the door, and when Mallory sees me cringe, she leads me to the passenger side and doesn't move until my seat belt is buckled.

After she gets in and starts the truck, she takes a deep breath and says: "Do you think he went home?"

I don't answer her at first, because I honestly hadn't thought about that. If we go back now and he's not there, then I have to answer not only for being out all night, but for losing Jake, too. At this point I have no idea what to say to my parents about either question without being completely honest.

"I don't think he would go home," I finally say, trying to believe it.

"So . . . where then?"

I look out into the empty parking lot. Before, when Jake was in high school—when he wasn't so bent—the possibilities would've been endless: parties, friends, football, and baseball games. It's just as endless now, of course, but there's no framework to lean on. No way to anticipate even the simplest of scenarios.

A security guard in a golf cart, yellow lights spinning

across the parking lot, pulls up to the driver's side of the truck and gets out. He shines a flashlight into the cab, the beam right in our eyes.

"You can't sit here," he says. His hair is tied in a long black ponytail, and he glares at us like somebody who doesn't get paid enough to deal with this sort of bullshit.

"He was a patient," Mallory says, motioning to me. "And then his brother ran off. About six-two. Short black hair. Beard. He was wearing—" She looks at me, and I tell the security guard about Jake's T-shirt, his pants. Mallory turns back to the guard and says, "Did you see him?"

"You two can't sit in the parking lot," he says again, tapping his flashlight on the side of the truck twice. Mallory cocks her head to the side, as if she didn't understand what he said.

"We're not *sitting* in the parking lot." Her voice breaks as she says it, straining to be polite. To not rip this guy's head off. "Like I said, we're trying to find his brother who's"— she pauses and then, less confidently, says—"sick."

The security guard leans his mouth close to a microphone clipped to his shoulder, pausing to consider us one last time before he presses a button and says, "Five-four, this is Lucien. I have a possible resist and detain."

Mallory explodes. *"Resist and detain?* What the hell are you talking about?"

The security guard jumps back, dropping his hands into a ready position. As if Mallory were going to come through the window. To be honest, she looks like she just might.

"Calm down," he says.

"I explained to you why we're sitting here. And now you're going to *detain* us?" She laughs. "Yeah, okay."

"Mallory," I say, but she ignores me. Everything she has is trained on this guy. I speak to him instead. "Hey, I'm sorry, sir, but we're going now. Right, Mallory?"

The security guard reaches forward, putting one hand on the truck and another on his mic. "Five-four, permission to detain subjects for trespassing."

Then he smiles. It's the smile that gets me.

"I just got stitches!" I point down to my leg, but he doesn't look. "How in the hell is that trespassing?"

"Loitering then."

"Are you fucking kidding me?"

Mallory makes another frustrated noise and hits the steering wheel. "Listen, mall cop, we're leaving. It will save us all the embarrassment. That way you can pretend that you were going to *detain* us and we can go on with our night. So, adios."

Lucien steps forward and says, "I can't let you do that."

It all happens in one quick motion. Mallory glances at me and smiles, really quickly, before slamming down the clutch and shifting into first gear, nearly bunny hopping the truck forward, as Lucien yells out. She skips second gear completely, putting us straight in third as we fly across the parking lot. I turn around and watch Lucien run a few steps before skidding to a stop and then racing back to his golf cart. We're already out of the parking lot before he gets there.

I keep checking behind us, fully expecting to see cops or at least Lucien's golf cart with its spinning yellow lights giving chase. But after a few blocks, when nobody appears, Mallory looks over at me and says, "Calm down, that guy's not doing anything."

"I'm not worried. But I do wish you hadn't gone at him."

"Am I the one who dropped an F-bomb on the guy? Uh-uh. So, jump off that pedestal, Bennett."

"Well . . ." I start to form an objection, but I can't. For a second, I almost lob out a lame joke, something like

"I don't think I should be jumping off of anything else tonight." It would be stupid, but she'd laugh; we'd laugh. Things would snap back to the way they were before. But then reality crashes into me, and of course all I can say is "I just want to find Jake."

Mallory turns right onto Fairgrove Church Road. In the distance is the interstate. Wilco, a gas station that surely has some of our fellow graduates hanging around its parking lot, smoking and pretending like they're not drinking beer, and a Waffle House dot either side of the road. She guns the engine, pushing us through a yellow light and at the last second skids into the parking lot of the Waffle House.

"Okay, first things first. I need to go to the bathroom, and I'm not going in that gas station. It's disgusting." She looks at the gas station, then back to the Waffle House. "Not that this is going to be much better. While I'm in there, call your brother. Keep calling him until he answers."

How many times has he ignored me, every attempt I've made since he came back? Why would a simple phone call make him respond? Mallory reaches over and puts a hand on my forearm.

"Just try. If he answers, great. We go pick him up, and this is all over. If he doesn't . . ." She trails off for a moment. "Well, we'll drive around until we find him. How far could he have gotten?"

Truthfully, probably not too far. It's not like he's in shape. A small belly has formed under his T-shirts, and his face looks subtly different. Like a blurry photograph. But we still didn't know which direction he had gone. We could drive all night and never find him, actually end up farther away from him than when we started.

Mallory reaches over and takes my phone from me. She scrolls down, pushes a button, and hands it back. I can hear it ringing as she says, "I'll only be a minute."

When Jake's voicemail greeting starts, I almost hang up. In the background, someone laughs as the recording starts. "This is Jake"—pause, more background laughter—"leave me a message." And then, just before the recording cuts off, Jake says, "You two are idiots." I have no idea who they are or why Jake didn't redo the whole thing, but he sounds happy in a way I didn't remember was possible. I keep dialing his number, and every time I listen to the whole thing.

Somebody hits the hood of my truck, and I jump.

Wayne's standing in front of me, arms spread wide and grinning like a fool. Sinclair gives me a nod.

"The prodigal son, back again!"

I don't immediately get out, both because of my leg and what I know is the reality of officially acknowledging Wayne's presence. It means pulling him in, letting him know about Jake. I finally open the door when he hits the hood again and says, "What the shit, Bennett!"

I lower myself out slowly, and Sinclair says, "Oh, hell. What happened to you?"

"It's nothing," I say.

"Shit. Did Will and his friends do this?" Wayne comes over and investigates my leg. "I swear to God I'll kill those preppy assholes."

"They didn't do it," I say. "I jumped off the River Road bridge."

Wayne looks surprised at first, but then he starts nodding, his smile brighter than the Waffle House sign behind him. "So it's gonna be *that* kind of night then. Hell, yes."

I should tell him he's wrong; it's not any kind of night. But I don't have the energy or the will to do it. I can't lie about why I jumped in the river, and I sure as hell can't tell him about the medals. So I let him stand there with his arms out, annoyed that he didn't get to jump off a bridge, too.

"This makes me twice as pissed that you left me up there with old bee-in-his-ass Steve," Wayne says. "That dude didn't calm down until Will finally showed up. I should've let you kick his ass."

"Will asked about you," Sinclair said.

"Yeah, looking all sad and shit," Wayne says, pantomiming a tear. "Broke my heart."

Mallory is coming out of the restaurant, pausing to stare at her phone. I talk quickly, hoping to end this conversation before she gets back to the truck.

"Will's fine. He's not going to do anything. He and Mallory—" I have no idea how to catch them up or explain Mallory's status.

"The way I hear it, she straight up knocked his dick in the dirt at Chris Jensen's party," Wayne says. "Are you sure you two aren't—" He makes an obscene gesture, and I shake my head.

"What the hell was *that*?" Mallory says, putting her phone in her pocket. "Got something stuck down there, Wayne?"

"Wanna find out?"

"That would be a disappointment for both of us."

Sinclair laughs, and, eventually so does Wayne.

"I asked your brother if you were still out raising hell," Wayne says to me. "But he was no help at all."

"Wait, you've seen Jake?" I ask.

"He was with Becky Patterson," Sinclair says. "Over at the Wilco."

"Becky *Patterson*," Wayne affirms, elbowing me in the side. "Your brother's living a charmed life, son."

"Did they leave?" I ask, trying to see past the trees that fence the Waffle House parking lot from the interstate. I turn to Mallory. "We need to go."

"Go?" Wayne says. "It's graduation. The hell you have to *go* anywhere. Besides, Sin was just about to buy me breakfast."

"I told you, I don't have any money," Sinclair says.

As they argue, I limp toward the door of the truck and am about to get in when Wayne runs up and says, "Whoa, whoa. Where you going, Bennett?"

"I don't want to ruin your graduation," I say, slowly getting in my seat. "But I need to find him. And I'm pretty sure Becky Patterson isn't going to be able to handle him."

Wayne giggles, elbowing Sinclair in the ribs a few times,

until Mallory says, "Really? Are you two years old?"

"Damn, everybody's so serious tonight," Wayne says. "Listen, I don't know what your brother's packing, but—"

Mallory sighs.

"Sorry. Jesus. You don't need to find him. I know where they're going. They're going to her house, son. Her *house*."

Mallory shakes her head, getting in the truck. Before she starts it, Wayne and Sinclair jump into the bed, hitting the roof twice. Mallory opens the sliding rear window and says, "Idiots. Get out."

"Like I'm going to sit here with Sinclair while you're off doing . . . well, whatever's got you all tangled. I ain't missing another bridge, okay? This is our last hurrah and shit."

Wayne hits the top of my truck and yells, "Deerfield, bitches!"

"Let them come," I say, trying to force the frustration out of my voice as she glares into the bed of the pickup. "It will take another fifteen minutes to get them out of the truck anyway. And we know where he is now. So let's just go."

Wayne's still hooting and hollering in the back, half drunk and shouting about adventures and destiny. When Mallory looks back one last time, I reach out and cautiously touch her hand.

"Or you could pull out really fast and hope they fall out," I say, smiling.

On cue, Sinclair leans down and sticks his head through the window. "Are we going or what?"

Mallory tries to scowl, but I see the smile peek through as she says, "Hold on, moron."

Deerfield is on top of a hill, a neighborhood filled with houses bigger than our school. The party Mallory and I left hours ago is still raging as she weaves through the maze of cars. People walk in the shadows, holding hands and hugging. Some of them lie on the lawns of the houses, only visible from their subtle movements and muffled giggles. Becky lives up ahead, on a small side street, which, since her house is the only one on the road, is a glorified driveway. Mallory cuts the lights and parks a few feet away from the entrance.

Wayne and Sinclair jump off the back of the truck. Wayne does a commando barrel roll and starts army crawling toward the house, which gets Sinclair laughing. He pops up and jogs over, drumming the side of my door.

"I don't think he's in there," Mallory says, motioning to the house. "I mean, wouldn't the lights be on?"

"Maybe," Wayne says, winking. "And maybe not."

"They could be at the party," Mallory says.

"He wouldn't go to a high school party." Not even when he was in high school, I think. Of course my mind fires right back at me: yeah, but he's not the same guy, remember?

"Maybe Wayne and Sinclair could go check the party," Mallory says. "And we can look around the house. Just in case?"

In the distance a song starts, and Wayne nods his approval, begins gyrating and grinding his body to the beat of the far-off music. He slowly makes his way toward Sinclair, still dancing.

"Get away from me," Sinclair says, laughing and holding Wayne back with both hands.

"I'm a party machine. A party animal. I live to get down."

He's still dancing, still moving to the beat, when Mallory gets out of the truck and nods for me to follow her. When I do, Wayne turns his attention—and his dancing—to me. "You're next, soldier boy."

Mallory steps in front of him, and for a second there's a flash of excitement on his face. But that dissolves quickly as soon as he realizes Mallory doesn't want anything bumped or grinded. "You'll hurt his leg. Go check out the party, and we'll meet up with you."

Wayne bops his head with the music, throws an arm around Sinclair. "And once we find your brother, then we're going to have some fun, right?"

Even though I don't want to, I nod my head and lie to Wayne.

"Yeah, man, whatever you want."

Wayne stares at me for a second before smiling, pulling Sinclair close, and giving him a kiss on the temple. "You ready for this shit, Sin?"

He gives another excited yelp as he and Sinclair start down the dark road, toward the party. When they're gone, I start my walk and hobble and stagger down the long driveway, neither me nor Mallory saying a word.

When we get to the end of the driveway, it's obvious nobody's in the house: no lights, no sounds. We walk around back, but Jake isn't on the porch. He isn't sitting on the abandoned swing set, left over from Becky's childhood. I want to be disappointed, but how can I be? How can I be surprised by anything now?

I walk over and sit on one of the swings, trying to think.

To rest my leg for a second. When Mallory comes and sits next to me, I don't say anything, just drift slowly from side to side in the swing, trying to come to grips with the fact that I probably won't find Jake again tonight.

Headlights fill the yard, and we both freeze. Mallory is poised to run, but then she looks at my leg and doesn't move. A man and woman get out of the car, both of them scowling. The man shakes his head as he goes toward the front of the house. The woman is an older version of Becky, the same straw-colored hair and thin build. She wipes her eyes before she disappears to the front of the house, too. They don't even look at the backyard.

I exhale, and Mallory goes to stand up again when lights in the house start popping on, each one higher than the last until the top floor comes alive and the whole house burns. There's a piano in their living room: black and polished in the corner. Pictures, pieces of art; the whole house could be from a magazine. My eyes drift to the kitchen, its matching silver appliances shining, and I nearly jump off the swing. Becky's mom is staring at us.

"Oh, shit. Oh, shit," Mallory says.

I expect Mrs. Patterson to scream, to call for her husband or even the police. There's a butcher's block of knives right next to her, another option. Instead, she wipes her eyes, blinking tears away.

I stand up, and Mallory tries to pull me back down. I lift up my hand, slowly at first, testing a hunch. I wave, but she doesn't respond. She can't see us.

The yelling starts again, Becky's dad at an epic level. Every word is audible: "That's right. I'm the bad guy. I'm always the bad guy. That's just perfect." When Mallory says my name, I flinch.

"Should we go to the party?"

"I guess," I say. As we walk away from the house, the yelling gets even louder, like somebody has turned up the volume. We're barely out of their yard, walking along the tree line that fences the neighborhood, when Mallory says, "I'm never getting married."

"Everybody fights," I say.

"Exactly," she says. "What's the point?"

I try to step around a hole and tweak my leg. I bend over and try to breathe through the pain. When I'm back upright, I don't know what else to say but "You'll probably end up here in Deerfield, married, with a Labrador. Just like everybody else."

She stops. "No, I won't."

"What?"

"I'm not going to end up here with a fucking dog. Okay?"

"Um, okay," I say, not sure why this is so contentious. Why she's getting all pissy about Deerfield. The garages here are nicer than the house either of us lives in. She curses under her breath and rubs the back of her neck.

"I'm sorry. I think I'm just tired." When her phone rings, she laughs and shakes her head. "Right on time."

"Hey, I appreciate your help. But maybe you should go home. I'll find him eventually, and I'm sure Wayne will drive me around. Then you can call Will and fix all of this."

She bites her lip, nods again. For a moment everything about Jake falls away. Mallory looks broken, the way Jake looked when he first came home. Like something is missing. "Are you okay?"

She nods again, two quick movements, and says, "I'm fine. I promise. Let's go to the party and find your brother."

But I don't move. She was always there for me, always willing to look past the idiotic things I did. She never cut me loose, not really. We were unconditional, and maybe we still are. Maybe that's something that never goes away no matter how poorly you maintain it.

"You don't look fine," I say. "You look like you should probably go home and sleep."

She forces a smile. "I can't leave you with those two dumbasses. You won't have working arms or legs by sunrise. Besides, Jake's probably at the party with Becky."

I try to believe it as we start walking again.

Mallory puts her arm around my shoulder as the sounds of the party get louder. It doesn't take a genius to see how her face is crimped and anxious. When her phone rings again, she pulls away to silence it, and when she does, I see the digitized picture of Will and Mallory smiling, a self-portrait of them in the mountains. Leaves—or maybe muted flowers?—swirl behind them. The screen dies, and Mallory sighs.

"So . . . why did you hit him?"

"You wouldn't believe me if I told you," she says.

"Try me."

She looks straight ahead, smiling sadly into the growing light from the party. She squeezes my shoulder once and says, "Not tonight. Okay?"

We move slowly because of my leg, but soon enough

we're on the porch of the house. People look past us, their party still going strong. I expected them to point, to relive Mallory's dramatic exit immediately upon our arrival. Instead, they drink and laugh with the same enthusiasm as earlier in the night.

"I'll go see if Jake's here," I say. "That way you don't have to go inside."

Mallory looks around the front lawn, the party having expanded outside the house. "I'd rather just come with you. Safety in numbers and all that."

She laughs weakly.

We don't get three steps inside the door when Wayne and Sinclair tumble through the crowd, pulling Becky Patterson behind them. My heart jumps. She's pretty and popular, and if you had asked me before I heard her parents fighting, I would've told you her life was perfect. Perfect clothes. Perfect hair. Perfect BMW convertible in the school parking lot. Perfect.

Wayne takes a swig of the beer he's holding. "Tell him."

"Your brother was acting like a total freak—no offense."

"Where is he now?" I ask.

"I left him at the Wilco. He started talking with Clem.

That guy who's always down there. He once told me—"
Wayne doesn't like the circular way she's telling the story
because he shakes his head and cuts her off.

"Your brother went with Clem," he says. "Do you
know him?"

"Nope," I say.

"He lives in a trailer out near Sherrills Ford," Wayne
says, taking a beat and another pull from the bottle. "I'm,
uh, surprised Jake knows him. He hangs out with my
brother and . . ."

Wayne looks like his beer has gone sour, a feeling I'm
trying to fight myself. Wayne's brother was a prick when
we were younger, the kind of guy who'd hold you down and
punch your arm until it went purple. Not much changed as
he got older. The last time I saw him he was beating a guy
unconscious in the parking lot of SuperMart. I'm pretty
sure he got thirty days in the county jail for it, too.

"Okay. So that means you know where Clem's trailer
is?" I ask. "Right?"

"Yeah, but—"

I turn to Mallory. "I can take you home first. Or you
can come with us. Whatever you want."

Before she can answer, Wayne steps closer to me, a hand

on my shoulder. "We're not going to Clem's. Forget that."

"Why not?" Mallory asks. "If Jake's there, we need to go get him."

"Yeah, I hear that, but"—he takes another drink of beer—"this ain't the kind of place where you just show up, you know? How about I call Jerry Lee and see if Jake's there."

Wayne pulls out his cell phone and dials a number. Whenever people pass by our circle, Mallory shoves her hands in her pockets and stares at the hardwood floors like it's her calling in life. Wayne pulls his phone from his ear, and I say, "Well?"

"No answer. But I can keep trying."

"You don't have to come," I say. "Just tell me where it's at."

Wayne looks at Sinclair, then Mallory before he levels his eyes on me. "I can't," he says. "I'm sorry."

He doesn't look confident as he says it, but when I open my mouth, he shakes his head and turns around as if he's going to disappear back into the party. As long as I've known Wayne, he's never been coy about anything. He's the hard charger, the guy most likely to get arrested for a public disturbance. The hesitation worries me even more because I really don't have any idea why Jake is out with this guy, but I can't focus on any of that. I shrug.

"Then I'll go down to Wilco and start asking people," I say. "Somebody's got to know him over there. I'll keep asking until I find out where he lives, man."

I spin around on my good leg and head for the door, but Wayne jumps in front of me, talking low. "Let me call Jerry Lee one more time. You don't know what you're getting into with this."

"You don't understand," I say, and my voice sounds too loud—as if everybody in the party can hear me. I lean closer to Wayne. "I have to find him, man. I can't leave him out there alone."

Wayne scratches the back of his neck and, in a moment of clear resignation, tosses his empty beer bottle at a recycling bin in the kitchen.

"Well, shit's about to get interesting." He points at me. "I'm the one who's going inside, and that's it, all right? We're getting your brother, and then we're leaving."

CHAPTER FOURTEEN

Wayne runs to get my truck while I wait with Mallory at the party. When he comes roaring up the street, I move as fast as I can to the passenger side, and Mallory climbs in the back with Sinclair. Whenever we stop at a light or slow down to make a turn, Wayne turns his head to the window like he's going to be sick.

We pull onto a gravel road, and the outlines of about five or six trailers are visible in the distance. A few have porch lights, and a large flat-screen television plays through the window of another. Normally Wayne would get on Sinclair, ask him if this felt like home. But he's dead quiet, nearly hanging his head out the window now.

"Clem's is the one at the back," he says, pulling the truck to the end of the long gravel road. I open my door at the same time as he does, and he looks over at me annoyed. "Hell, no. You're staying in the truck."

Wayne's big, the nose tackle on the football team. He could easily put me down, leg or not, even if I could rush for the door. But Jake is my brother, and I'm the one who's supposed to bring him home.

"He won't know who you are," I say. Whether it's true or not, I can't say. But I set my face, trying to convince him.

"You're not hearing me," he says.

"You're right, I'm not," I say, trying to get out of the truck.

Mallory calls my name from the back. "Maybe you should let Wayne go. If Jake's in there, he'll find him."

"I need to do this," I say, ending the conversation as I lower myself carefully to the ground, ignoring Wayne's cussing. When we're standing in front of the truck, I put my hand on his shoulder. "In and out, I swear."

The trailer is set off from the rest of the park. Its windows are papered in thick black, and the yard is littered with metal folding chairs. Half an engine is propped up on cinder blocks, and a grill, covered with beer bottles, is filled with dirty water. The whole place smells like eggs. Before we come up on the porch, Wayne stops me.

"Thomas, for real, these guys aren't the type who like dudes just showing up." He hesitates and says, "So don't look at anything, don't say anything. No matter what. Cool?"

I nod, and Wayne steels himself, making fists with his hands and then releasing them. He breathes deeply once before knocking on the door, a flimsy, almost cardboard thing that shudders with each rap. Nobody answers right away, and I'm about to push in front of him and knock louder, harder when the door flies open.

Jerry Lee, who looks like Wayne, but with a sharper face and a shaved head, appears in front of us. When he sees Wayne, he grabs him by the neck and drives us both off the porch. The pain is like a spike in my leg as I try to keep myself from falling in the dirt. A large dog runs to the door, barely getting past the frame before a piece of plastic cord jerks him back inside. He goes nuts as Wayne stumbles to his feet and pushes his brother.

"What the fuck, Jerry Lee?"

"Me? The hell *you* doing here?"

"We're looking for his brother, jackass," Wayne says.

Jerry Lee stares at me, wiping his nose with the side of his hand. "And who the hell are you?"

"He's—" Jerry Lee cuffs Wayne on the side of his head once, laughing when Wayne raises up like he's about to throw a punch.

"I didn't ask you." He turns back to me. "Well?"

"Thomas Bennett."

Jerry Lee gives a theatrical laugh. "Oh, shit, soldier boy's your brother?"

I take a step toward the porch—I'll push my way through the door if I have to—but Wayne stops me with a look. It's angry but mixed with something else I don't at first recognize: fear. He holds his hand out, like he's approaching a wild dog. "Becky Patterson told us he went with Clem, so I thought—"

"You thought? Nah, you didn't think," his brother says. "If you were thinking, you wouldn't have brought him here."

Wayne shakes his head but doesn't respond. I try to look past Jerry Lee, into the trailer. When I do, he jumps toward me. "Where the hell do you think you're going?"

"I want to talk to Clem," I say.

As soon as I say the words, Wayne groans.

Jerry Lee looks at Wayne and shakes his head. "You're a goddamn idiot. But fine. You guys want to talk to Clem? All right, let's go talk to Clem."

He holds the door open without ceremony. I limp past him, but Wayne hesitates, only following after Jerry Lee starts to leave him outside. The trailer is small, a long rectangle of rooms stacked side by side like a railroad car. The dog drops its head and walks toward us, whining. When neither of us reaches for it, it turns around and lies down on a dirty pillow underneath the window air conditioner unit. Everything in the room is on: the television, the microwave, every light in the small trailer.

"Clem's in the back," Jerry Lee says. Wayne tries to follow me, but Jerry Lee stops him. "You're not looking for your brother. Sit down."

He points to a ripped-up couch, covered in dog hair, and then points me down the hallway. "Go on."

I follow the hallway and slide open a fake wood door when I reach the end. A skinny shirtless man is sitting on the bed, arranging the contents of a large gray cooler at his feet. Plastic tubing. A bottle of starting fluid. And boxes upon boxes of what looks like cold medicine.

Clem looks up but isn't surprised to see me standing there. Two bulldogs, like sentries, draw blood just below his collarbones, and something in old English is inked across his stomach. A silver cross hangs from his neck.

"Well?" He closes the cooler and looks at me.

"I'm looking for Jake Bennett."

Clem doesn't act like he knows Jake. He stands up, puts a foot on the cooler, and stares at me. "Am I supposed to know you?"

"I'm Thomas, his brother."

"Okay, Thomas. But why are you here?"

Emotions collide. Why is Jake hanging with Clem? How does he even know this guy? I study the carpet, dotted with stains. "Just tell me where he is, and I'll leave."

Clem bends down but doesn't answer. He grabs a small Thermos and sticks it in the cooler. "Why do you think I know where your brother is?"

"You were with him."

"Correction," Clem says. "He asked me for a ride, and I gave him one."

When he stands up from the bed, I'm spinning the pieces of what's happening in my head, trying to make them fit. Clem goes to his closet and pulls out a length of rope, wrapping it around his closed fist in big loops before setting it on top of the cooler.

"Well, did you bring him back here?"

Clem slams his hand down hard on the cooler. "Am I your brother's fucking baby-sitter?"

When I don't answer him, he picks up one side of the cooler and pulls it out of the room, leaving me there. I don't immediately follow him, but when I hear a crash in the living room, followed by yelling, I stumble out of the room and up the hallway as quickly as I can. By the time I get outside, Wayne and Jerry Lee are on the ground, wrestling. Mallory and Sin are standing just outside the porch, both of them taking cautious steps toward the melee as if they want to break it up. Wayne spins and ends up on top of Jerry Lee, pushing his forearm into his brother's throat. At the last second Jerry Lee pivots his hips and throws Wayne off. Before Wayne can get close again, Jerry Lee pulls a large knife from the back of his jeans and points it at Wayne like a gun.

"This is your fault," Jerry Lee says, breathing hard. "What the fuck are you thinking, bringing all these people here? Soldier boy's brother is bad enough, but I come out here and you've got two more sitting in this truck? Hell, no. You got to learn a lesson."

"Good lesson, genius." Mallory looks angrier than I've ever seen her. "Because now we're all stuck here."

"Y'all's feet work just fine, I'm sure," he says.

"You want us to walk?" Mallory says. "It's ten miles back to town!"

"Walk?" I say. But as soon as the words come out of my mouth, I see the way my tires have sunk to the ground, four puddles of empty rubber. "What the hell?"

I take a step toward Jerry Lee, but Wayne moves between us, putting his hands against my chest. "Just tires, man. Just tires."

And I know. But everything about tonight comes rushing into my body like a wild animal. It's Jake's not being here. My dad. The frustration of never being in control, ever. And now this. My body won't stop shaking.

Wayne is in my ear. "Not worth it. All right? Just tires."

Jerry Lee smiles as he wipes the blade on his shorts. "You should've had more sense than this, Wayne. Coming around here and expecting there wouldn't be consequences. And now I've got myself a brand-new truck for the trouble. So maybe I should thank you?"

"New truck?" I repeat.

I fight through the pain, taking step after step until I'm right in Jerry Lee's face. I wish I could take the knife from him, could twist it out of his hands, and put him on the ground the way I've seen it done in the movies. How many times? Instead, I push him. As hard as I can. He stumbles backward, smiles.

"Big balls on this kid," he says to Wayne.

"You'll see how big if you don't fix my truck," I say.

Before Jerry Lee can say anything, Clem strides from behind the trailer, his scarecrow chest still shirtless. When he sees everybody, the truck in the distance, he says, "The hell is going on out here, Jerry Lee? And put that damn knife away. What if a sheriff's deputy comes driving by and sees that Rambo-ass thing?"

I refuse to break eye contact as I speak, my heart like a jackrabbit.

"He cut my tires."

"And he was about to come at me," Jerry Lee says. "If he's man enough."

Clem gives Jerry Lee an annoyed look. Shakes his head. "Will you shut the hell up? What were you thinking?"

When he turns back to me, his smile isn't friendly. "Now get the fuck out of here."

Jerry Lee laughs, even harder when I take a few steps at Clem and my leg buckles underneath me. Clem doesn't laugh, just stares at me coldly. Mallory steps forward, talking directly to Clem.

"We can't walk home, not with his leg."

Clem's eyes flash, just for a second, as he looks around the gravel road. "You guys come here uninvited. Walk into my house, asking questions and making demands. And now this?" He turns to Wayne. "Get your friends the fuck out of here before I really do something."

Wayne doesn't wait for another word. He comes over to Mallory and Sinclair, trying to corral them. But I don't move. "What about my truck?"

Clem covers the five feet between us in two steps. He's right in my face, his breath like old cheese. But before he can say or do anything—and God, I'm so ready for somebody to finally give me permission to let go, to get unhinged—I hear my name.

Jake's coming down the driveway toward us. At first I can't believe it. He's so thin, so pale that he must be a ghost. But then he says my name again, and I snap out of the dream.

"What are you doing here?" he asks.

"Me? Are you kidding?"

"Get this kid out of here," Clem says to Jake. "For real."

Jake tries to grab my arm, but I push him away.

"Hell, no. I'm not leaving," I say. "You left me in the hospital! Do you realize how long I've been looking for you?"

Jake tries to pull me away, but I put all my weight into my good leg. He can still drag me forward, but it takes some effort. Behind us, Mallory, Wayne, and Sinclair watch us. Normally I'd be embarrassed, I'd want to take Jake to the side of the trailer so nobody could see this happening. But fuck it, I won't hide anything for him anymore.

"Let's go," he says, loudly, once again trying to guide me away from Clem. It's a momentary flare of his former self, something that I know won't last.

"Look what they did to the truck. Do you even care?"

Jake turns for a second, considering the wheels. He used to love that truck as much as I do. The day he turned sixteen and Dad gave him the keys, there wasn't a happier person in all of North Carolina. Now he only shrugs.

Shrugs.

And that's it.

I pull away from him and walk up the gravel driveway,

toward the road. I keep walking, ignoring the pain in my leg and Mallory, who's chasing after me, calling my name. Jerry Lee yells out, "Don't worry, I'll take good care of your truck."

But I don't care.

I don't care about the truck or Jerry Lee's laughter. I don't care about Mallory, pleading with me to stop, worrying about my stitches, and the tears of anger and pain coming down my cheeks. I don't worry about Jake, who doesn't jog to catch up even though I'm halfway out of the trailer park by the time he takes his first step. I'll walk all the way across this country if I have to. And there's not a damn thing Jake or anybody else is going to do about it.

CHAPTER FIFTEEN

We've walked for what feels like miles, and Jake still hasn't caught up. He's fifty feet behind us, hands in his pockets, slow as time. None of us speak except for Wayne, who does nothing but curse Jerry Lee.

Fuck.

I don't know how I'm going to get the truck back, let alone fixed. I have no idea what time it is or how I'm even going to get home before the sun comes up. And that doesn't even begin to touch on Jake. It all hangs over me, pulling me down like a drowning man.

Fuck, fuck, *fuck*.

Each step is awful, like someone has packed broken

glass under my skin. I'm trying not to limp because I know Mallory is worried and watching me. She's been intentionally slowing the pace of the group for the past mile, and I'm still lagging. But I don't want to give Jake the satisfaction of . . . what? Knowing that I'm in pain? I have no idea why that matters, but I march forward, barely blinking.

When we come to Highway 10, Mallory's had enough. She jumps out in front of the group, stopping us.

"Okay, this is ridiculous," she says. "You can't keep this up."

"I'm fine," I say, trying to keep moving. She blocks me easily with a hand to my chest and then bends down to check my leg. The stitches are still in place, but it feels swollen. And now that we've stopped, the pain is nearly unbearable. It's all I can do to not scream when she accidentally causes me to shift my weight to my bad leg.

"We need to call someone," she says to Wayne and Sinclair.

Everybody we know is at a party or halfway to the beach by now. Or drunk. But Sinclair and Wayne still brainstorm a list. Every number they call follows the same pattern. Dial, listen for a few seconds, followed almost immediately by some intense cussing when nobody answers. They've gone through almost ten numbers when Jake finally jogs up.

"What's going on?" he says.

Mallory drops her hands to her sides. "Are you serious? Look at his leg."

Jake bends down to inspect my leg the same way Mallory did and says, "I've walked on worse."

"You've walked on worse? Are you *kidding*?"

A peculiar look of nostalgia comes over Jake as he talks, completely ignoring Mallory's indignation. The knives in her eyes.

"You remember that, Thomas? When I cut my toe with the lawn mower? Nearly took the whole thing off."

It had looked like hamburger, but we walked back to our house, him trailing blood down the sidewalk and me freaking out. That was the summer we were supposed to mow lawns together. The summer before Jake's junior year. The money was going toward the truck, which needed a new axle and—if there was money left over—a bed liner. I mowed all summer without him, getting the axle, the bed liner—and a new set of tires.

But I don't want to think about the truck or engage Jake's sudden nostalgia trip. I refuse to look at him as I step around Mallory and start down the road again.

"We could call your parents," she says, easily matching my shortened stride.

I want to fight. It would feel *good* to fight, to be loud and truthful. But I tamp down the urge to bring out the claws. And besides, Mallory isn't the problem. I slow down and face her.

"I can't explain this to them. Not tonight. Okay?"

I can tell she doesn't want to concede the point, but she finally sighs and says, "As long as we can agree that you're being an idiot right now."

She smiles, almost embarrassed. Before I can say anything else, Jake surges past us like we're not even there, Wayne and Sinclair in tow.

"That's the best team Ford's had in twenty years," Jake tells Wayne. "Me, Teague, Wagner—Bryant? If it wasn't for that bullshit call, we take State."

He marches them down the road like they've got orders, taking the lead for the first time in months. I try to keep up, to hear what he's saying. To maybe figure out how he can go from mute to discussing high school football legacies with such ease.

I've pulled ahead of Mallory by a few steps, but I can't

keep up with Jake. The last thing I hear is Wayne saying, "Bulllsshhhiiitt," loud and with feeling. Followed by laughter that carries through the dark country night.

The next sound is Mallory's phone.

"Is that Will?" I ask, pausing to wait for her.

"Of course," she says. When it beeps again, she nods and types out a quick message before looking back up at me. At my leg. She grimaces. "I know you don't want to hear it, but—"

I shake my head. "I can't call them."

And yes, every step is a warning—infection, paralysis, worse. I've been so careful up until tonight about not risking anything. And in less than a few hours I've resurrected my friendship with Mallory, lost the practical use of one leg and now my truck.

What can a five-mile walk possibly do to me now?

"Something's going on with you," Mallory says.

"It's Jake," I say, trying to shore up any emotion leaking into my face. Act like nothing is wrong. Be cool, I tell myself. Look at peace. But Mallory doesn't buy it. She stops walking and gently pulls my arm until I stop, too.

"I've known you for how long? And you're going to lie to my face?"

"I'm not lying to you," I say. But I can't look her in the eyes when I say it. Even if I wanted to tell her, what are the words? Even after everything we've done tonight, I still can't explain what I'm feeling, what I'm planning for tomorrow. And of all the failures between me and her, this one might be the biggest.

When I look up, I say, "It's complicated."

She nods, as if I've dropped some serious philosophy on her. "I'm good at complicated. Trust me."

I try to look away again, but she won't let me. "Seriously, Bennett. You can tell me anything. You have to know that."

The words slice me up, and her eyes are equally sharp, cutting through every defense I have. She stares at me, neither of us moving as Jake, Wayne, and Sinclair get farther and farther away.

I'm so tired. Of this night. Of every single lie I've told. All of it. And when I hear Jake laugh—so loud, so clear—I don't weigh it. I don't plan it.

I say it out loud for the first time.

"I'm not going to the army."

She doesn't respond at first, and I worry that she didn't understand. I don't want to look at her because I can't take seeing even the smallest amount of disappointment on her face. I stare at the long road in front of us, immediately regretting telling her.

But then she asks, "Why?"

And I say, "I can't come back like Jake."

It feels weird saying the words, as if I'm finally giving them life. And now that they're upright and moving, I realize that I can no longer control them. They'll run across the countryside, ravaging villages. It makes my truck's immobilization hurt worse than my leg, a heavy reality that sits on my shoulders.

I still can't read Mallory's face or her tone as she says, "Are you going to get in trouble? Like, with the government?"

"I haven't shipped yet. I can still get out of it," I say, but even those words seem wrong. It's not a technicality I'm breaking. It's a commitment that goes far beyond how many times I've actually signed my name.

And if anybody knows this better than I do, it's Mallory. She closes her eyes and asks the question that scares me most of all: "What about your dad?"

I could call and wake up the recruiter right now. Despite all the bowling trips, the pizza, the rah-rah meetings.

There's no loyalty to him or the clipboard he used to sign me up. And if I'm honest, I can even deal with putting my head down and walking past all the people in this town who thought I was brave, a hero. But telling my dad is completely different.

"I guess he'll figure it out when the recruiter calls," I say.

She thinks about this for a few seconds and then says, "Are you sure you want to do that?"

"What else can I do?"

"You could tell him," she says.

"Oh, yeah. That would go over amazingly, I'm sure."

"So that's it? You just . . . leave?" Mallory looks up and down the road, as if she were waiting for somebody. "That doesn't sound like you. At all."

It's a knockout punch, and my hands are down. Everybody—even Mallory—thinks I'm something I'm not. But I don't know how to stop what I've set in motion at this point. Not that there's much of a plan left. By the time I can get back to the truck, it will be either gone or completely stripped down to the frame, the parts sold. So not only do I have to walk into the living room and tell Dad I'm not going to the army, I also get to tell him I lost the truck. I can see the disappointment form in his face, the lines creasing his forehead. He'll grab me by the elbow and force me into the car. We won't stop until I'm standing outside the recruiting station, a rucksack in one hand and a bus ticket in the other.

I glance at Mallory unsure of what I'll see, what she'll say to me. And at first she isn't showing me anything. Her face is absent of emotion, and her mouth is open, just a little bit. But then the tension in her face breaks.

"You don't have to leave," she says. "You changed your mind. People do it every day."

I want to believe her, but I stepped off the path a long time ago. And I have no idea how to get back on it. I have no idea how I can fix any of this. Mallory takes my hand.

"We could talk to your mom and dad: you and me." Her voice is emotional, adamant. "Everybody should be able to change their mind, Thomas. We can do this if you want to. Right now."

Ahead of us, Jake has stopped walking. From this distance he almost looks normal. I turn to Mallory and say, "It doesn't even matter anymore. Without the truck, I'm done."

Wayne yells something at us, but I can't make it out;

they're too far away. They head back, and Mallory jabs a thumb at the trees that line the road. "Our only option is to live in the woods then. You like squirrel? I bet you'd look awesome with a beard." She bumps her shoulder into mine. "Don't need a truck for that."

That smile. I can feel it in my chest. I've been missing it for seven years. Having somebody who would walk into traffic for me. She pulls me close to her, into a hug that seems to last forever. I feel her phone buzzing in her pocket, but she ignores it, only letting go of me when the headlights from a passenger van peek up over the oncoming hill, filling the dark night with light.

It's a church van, FIRST BAPTIST printed on the side in electric blue. When Mallory sees the van, she goes stiff, barely moving her lips as she speaks.

"Remember, I did this for you."

Will opens the door of the van and jumps down. Wayne and Sinclair are throwing their hands in the air like the Lord has answered a prayer, sent a boat to escape the Flood. When they see Will, they stop. Sinclair hides his face below his NASCAR hat, and all Wayne says is "Damn."

Jake jogs up to the back of the van, thanking Will as

he climbs in and sits in the backseat. Wayne and Sinclair
follow suit, but neither me nor Mallory moves. Will looks
at me, then Mallory and shakes his head. When he does
it, Mallory makes like she's going to go to him but stops
herself. For the first time I see the depth of Mallory's pain
as her eyes search his face.

"Will—" she says.

"Just get in the van," he says, turning his back on us.

Mallory looks at the ground and mumbles, "I didn't
know who else to ask. I'm sorry, but you can't walk home
on that leg."

The van comes to life in a low rumble, and I look at
Will, staring straight ahead. "I don't think he wants to
give me a ride."

"Well, yeah. Probably not. But you're the reason I asked
him. So it's not like I'm going to let him leave you here."

I should grab her and disappear into the woods. Take
her to the Grover, become the next urban legend, the crazy
friends who disappeared on graduation night. Ghosts.
Psychos. Don't ever go in there, man. That's the *real* story.
At the very least, I should thank her because when's the
last time anybody's done something like this for me?

"So this is it," I say.

"For tonight." Will honks the horn, and Mallory sighs. "All right, you ready for this?"

I look at the van and so does she, and without a word, we both climb in.

I'm in the back row with Jake, the smell of cigarettes and beer coming off Sinclair and Wayne. Sunday, when a pack of Baptists hops in their van, they'll find it marinated in sin. The only sound is the hum of the tires. Nobody talks, and Will doesn't turn on the radio. Mallory sits in the passenger seat, but she and Will couldn't be farther apart. Every time Mallory tries to say something to him, he turns away, as if staring out the window will increase their separation. More than once I catch him staring at me in the rearview mirror.

Fifteen minutes later we're downtown. Five more, and Will has the van parked at the Waffle House. Wayne's truck is still there from what seems like hours ago. Now Will and Mallory will fade away together, and I'll be left to figure out what to do with Jake, with the rest of my life. I'm barely out of the van when Will comes rushing toward me.

He looks me right in the eye and says, "So I guess you found Mallory, huh?"

"Okay, man," I say, starting away from the group; this isn't going to end well for anyone. He comes charging again and pushes me into the Waffle House window.

"Just a friend, right?" he says.

"Will, stop." Mallory grabs him by the arm, but he only gets in my face closer, louder.

"I was trying to help her out," I say. "I told you to leave her alone for the night."

"So you can make your move? Right." He looks at Mallory and says, "Is this why you did it?"

When I try to slip away from him, he pushes me back into the glass, harder this time. Behind me, I can feel the people in the Waffle House staring at us. I swallow my own anger, the desire to push him back.

"Is he why you did it?" Will asks Mallory again, louder this time. He turns back to me, finger in my face. "You were probably in on it the whole time. You're a fucking coward, Thomas."

I don't really see what happens next, but Will goes flying backward. Jake falls on top of him and starts yelling about respect and how Will doesn't know the first thing about honor or courage. Will keeps trying to turn away from Jake—his eyes wide with fear—but Jake grabs his chin and forces him to make eye contact.

"Call my brother a coward? The night before he goes in? Are you fucking crazy? I'd kill you for less."

Will looks terrified as Jake pins him harder against the ground. And he should be worried. I've never seen Jake so—so out of control.

"Thomas, do something!" Mallory screams, pushing me toward Jake. But how do I stop this? How can I do anything for Jake? I try to pull him off, but Jake shoves me away.

"Hell, no, Thomas. He can't do this, not after everything I've tried to do to keep you safe."

I don't have a chance to figure out what Jake has done for me; how he could possibly think he's kept me *safe*.

"Let him go," Mallory yells, trying to pull Jake off Will. But he's on a mission, singular in his focus.

"You're going to apologize," Jake tells Will, raising a fist. Mallory screams again, and Will starts talking fast.

"I'm sorry, I'm *sorry*. But what do you expect me to do? She's out with him all night, and I don't even get a reason." Will turns his head to face me, pleading. "We're supposed to get married tomorrow, man. And then she tells me it's not happening; just like that, it's over. And then she spends all night with you."

Time—the world—stops moving. Even Jake looks at me. Mallory's face is as blank with shock.

"What was I supposed to do?" he says.

Jake returns his focus to Will. "That doesn't excuse shit."

He puts his fist in the air, and Will closes his eyes, bracing for the impact. Before he can throw a punch, Wayne tackles Jake, followed by Sinclair. I'm still trying to process everything as Jake brushes them aside and starts back at Will.

Wayne yells my name, waking me up. "Get Jake the hell out of here. Now!"

Jake picks Will up off the concrete, both fists in his shirt as he pushes him against the window. Will keeps repeating the same word—*please* —over and over again. Mallory runs to Jake, trying to get Will loose, but he ignores her, too.

"Jake," I say. Then again, louder. When I put my hand on his shoulder, he spins around with his fist raised.

"Leave him alone," I say.

"Hell, no. This doesn't happen," he says. "Not tonight.

Not right before you go in. Not when I haven't taken care of *this*."

He shakes his backpack in my face, as if proving a point. When he turns back to Will, I grab the backpack off his shoulder.

"What the *hell* is this?" When I go to open it, he spins around and pushes me hard.

"Drop it!" His eyes go from anger to panic, and when I don't answer him, when I start to open the backpack, he hits me. One shot to my eye, like a strike of lightning.

Will bolts away from the restaurant, grabbing Mallory and making a run for the church van. When he gets the van started, they peel out of the small parking lot. I expect Jake to chase them onto the highway, into the night. Instead, he spits, picks up the backpack, and then walks inside the restaurant.

CHAPTER SIXTEEN

I try convincing myself to start walking again. Walk until the sun comes up, until I hit the state line. If it weren't for my leg, I would, I tell myself. So I lean against the side of the building, refusing to look through the windows at Jake or Wayne or Sinclair.

Wayne comes outside and hands me a washrag filled with ice. "For the eye," he says.

He works a toothpick between his teeth for a minute before saying, "Okay, so Jake calmed down. It's all I could do to keep that waitress from calling the law, let alone get Jake to sit down. I think you should probably come in there and talk to him."

"He can go to hell," I say, carefully putting the ice against my eye. It will be black, that's certain. And only now, as the adrenaline is beginning to wear off, do I feel the pain. The weight of Jake's fist against my face. How pissed I actually am.

Wayne cocks his head to the side. "Yeah, well—" He pauses and then says, "How about I drive you guys somewhere?"

I make myself turn and look at Jake over my shoulder. He's sitting across from Sinclair, stiff as a board. Same as always. It's like he turned off the power, which gets my blood going even more. There's nothing I could do—punch through the glass, jump into traffic—that would even register with him right now.

"Fuck this," I say, trying to stand up. The combined pain from my leg and eye makes me nauseated. Wayne says something else about Jake, but it barely registers. I have no idea what I'm going to do now or why I even cared about what was happening with Jake. I should've joined the chorus of our family, the rest of this town: he'll be fine. Don't worry.

I drag myself over to the side of the building, where nobody can see me, and throw up. Wayne comes running up behind me.

"Shit, are you okay?"

I fall back against the building, my body hot on the bricks as I lean my head back. Along with all the food, the water, I got rid of any fight I have left. I'm done.

The door opens, and I still think I'm going to hear a voice from the past. Jake telling me to get up, to be tough. All the same bullshit. Instead, a woman speaks.

"He's not drunk, is he?" the waitress asks. "Because if he is, you guys need to go. I should've called the cops when they started fighting."

"I'm not drunk," I say.

This is an all-natural debilitation. To think you don't even need to drink or do drugs to feel so shitty, so helpless. As if to convince her, I look up and try to smile with conviction. Anything to get her back inside the restaurant.

"He really got you," she says. "I can still call the cops if you want."

I shake my head, everything spinning. "No. He's my brother."

The waitress looks confused for a second but then says, "Was it about that girl?"

I can't help myself, I laugh. "No."

And for a second it's like Jake isn't sitting in the

restaurant—a robot, a mannequin—and suddenly it's only Mallory. Mallory, who's getting married. Who's spent the last months, all night, pretending, just like me. I don't know if I should be angry or impressed by the fact that we both are so good at it.

The waitress gives me another strange look, sighs. "Well, if you're not drunk and you promise there won't be any more fights"—she motions to the restaurant—"then come inside and get some food. You probably need it."

"Thanks," Wayne says, winking. "Is that on the house, good-looking guy discount?"

The waitress doesn't turn around as she says, "It's full price, the dumbass high school boy special."

Wayne chuckles to himself. He sits down against the building and rubs his hands together. My stomach rumbles, from hunger or sickness. Wayne looks over his shoulder, up through the glass windows of the restaurant.

"She's going to give us a discount," he says. "Trust me."

I don't say anything, and Wayne keeps rubbing his hands together nervously. He starts and stops a few sentences before sighing and finally saying, "So, you and Mallory. You're not hitting that, right?"

"No," I say.

Wayne looks relieved. "Okay, at least this isn't *really* fucked up. I mean, it's definitely fucked up. But if you and her were getting it on?" He shakes his head. "They're getting *married*."

When I don't engage, he goes back to rubbing his hands and sighing. "Listen, I realize you and Jake aren't exactly down with each other right now. But I can't leave him here. What happens if he, um, well, you know? Freaks out again."

Then he'll have to deal with the consequences. Or even better, Mom and Dad will have to deal with it. But at what cost? I look into the restaurant. It's full of men and women in blue work shirts, their names stitched above their pockets, all of them from the hosiery mill two blocks north of here. Most look older than they should, cracked and worn under the fluorescent lighting. Some laugh; others pull unlit cigarettes from half-empty packs sitting on the table, bringing them to their lips by habit. Every one of them looks tired, and not because they work the swing shift. It's the kind of tired I've felt for months, the kind that doesn't go away no matter how much you sleep.

Wayne studies my face before clapping his hands together. "Well, hell. I need some food to soak up all this alcohol. What do you say?"

Wayne stands up and, offering me his hand, pulls me to my feet. Inside, Jake is ignoring a plate of eggs. Maybe Sinclair ordered them, or maybe the waitress just brought them out. Either way, it doesn't matter. If this is how he wants to be, that's on him. I can't hold any of this together, and I'm not going to try anymore.

"I don't want to eat," I say. "Let's get him in the truck and get out of here, okay?"

Wayne nods and takes a step toward the restaurant as I limp behind him. Before we walk in the door, Wayne stops me. He looks inside, then back to me.

"So, this is all because of the war? I guess I didn't realize it was that bad, but when he went after Will? When he hit you? Damn." He moves when a truck driver and his wife come through the door. Wayne smiles at both of them, nodding until they're out of earshot.

"I don't care what's wrong with him," I say, and the muscles in my stomach clench. "He's fucked up, and I guess that's the end of it."

"What are you going to do?" he asks.

"Nothing. What can I do?"

The bluntness, the flat way the words come from my mouth, surprises Wayne. "What about your parents?

Are they going to do something?"

"What do you expect them to do?" I ask. "What would happen if Jake had to go to the head doctor? What would people say? Suddenly he's not Jake the hero. He's Jake, guy who beats people up in the parking lot of the Waffle House."

Wayne looks away, picking at some dead skin on the side of his thumb. My instinct is to apologize, to couch my sudden honesty with a reassurance that yes, everything will be okay. Jake will be okay. But I don't want to do that anymore. And more important: I don't know if it's true.

"Let's just go and get him," I say.

I limp into the restaurant, and a guy in the corner, drunk off his ass, stands up and starts clapping. He throws a few punches before falling back into his booth, laughing it up with his friends. When I get to Jake and Sinclair, I don't sit down.

"We're going home," I say.

Jake stares at his eggs, and it pisses me off. He rubs his face, and it pisses me off. I grab him by the arm and try to pull him out of the booth. When he puts his hand up, I'm ready for him. I want him to try to hit me again.

"Whoa, whoa!" Wayne jumps between us, pushing me down beside Sinclair, who nearly chokes on a piece of sausage as he tries to get out of the way. Wayne turns to the waitress, holding up both hands as he says, "They're just playing around, I promise."

She gives us one last look before turning to a group of men sitting at a table across the restaurant. Wayne sits next to Jake, the smile slowly falling away from his lips. "What the hell is your problem?"

I don't know if he's talking to Jake or me, but it doesn't matter because neither of us answers him. I don't take my eyes off Jake, daring him to look me in the eye. To explain even half of what happened tonight.

"You've got nothing to say?" I ask Jake. He doesn't look up, just plays with the paper napkin on the table. I pull it away from him. "You're seriously going to sit here and not say anything?"

Jake's eyes dart to mine as Wayne says, "Thomas, c'mon."

I ignore him. "I'm tired of this bullshit, Jake. I'm tired of covering for you every single time people ask how you're doing. Every time they get a glimpse of how fucked up you are. Do you realize how exhausting that is?"

Nothing. He picks a scab on his knuckle, expressionless. I slam my hands on the table, rattling the plates and
the sugar caddy, the windows, it seems. Everybody in the
restaurant looks at us, but I don't care.

"And what were you doing over at Clem's?" I ask, my
voice growing louder. A couple of guys in the corner stand
up and start walking toward us. "Can you answer that?
Can you say *anything*?"

Jake looks up, his face clear and angry. Like he's going
to take another swing. Before he can swing or speak, a
man wearing a VFW hat covered in brass and silver pins,
easily old enough to be my grandfather, puts a hand on
my shoulder and says, "Y'all are getting kind of loud over
here."

I try to shrug him away, but his grip is iron. "My friend
and I are trying to have a conversation, and all we can hear
is you fellas carrying on."

"You know what?" I turn and face the man, to tell
him exactly what he can do with his complaints. But as
soon as I move, he locks his hand harder on my shoulder.
Immediately Jake is up and trying to get past Wayne. The
man laughs.

"Boy, you better sit back down. You don't even know

the shit I've been through in my life." He holds out his free hand. "Semper Fidelis" is tattooed in slick black ink across his forearm. "If you don't know what that represents, I'll be happy to give you a free lesson."

Jake pauses, and for a second I think he's going to jump over the table. If the man didn't have me in such a vise, I'd already be between them. Jake rolls up his sleeve, all the way to the shoulder. And I can't believe it. Or maybe I can, but the tattoo is still shocking. The words are done in thick block text: "Death Before Dishonor."

The man laughs once. "A soldier? What, were the marines not recruiting the day you decided to join?"

"Nope," Jake says with a casualness I haven't heard from him in months. "I just wanted to be with the real men."

The man smiles bigger this time. "Well, it could be worse. You could be air force."

They both laugh. The man turns and yells to the waitress, "Doreen, Ray and I are going to pull our table over here. You good with that?"

The waitress nods, but her eyes flit over all of us nervously. Whether that's because of us or them I don't know. When VFW Hat's friend stands up, he's got a prosthetic leg underneath his jean shorts. He's maybe ten years older than Jake. They're both wearing the same blue work shirt with "Hickory Hosiery" stitched on the chest.

"This is Ray, second Iraq," VFW Hat says. The man smiles but doesn't say anything or reach a hand out. "I'm Phil, Vietnam."

The waitress brings a pot of coffee and six cups to the table, but Phil shakes his head. "Leave the cups, but you can take that coffee away." He pulls a mason jar from his coat and puts it on the table. As soon as Doreen sees it, she shakes her head.

"Do you want to get arrested?" she asks. "What if Brickwell shows up?"

Phil ignores her, telling us: "Lawman. Good dude. But probably wouldn't be too happy seeing a jar of 'shine on the table." He shakes the mason jar's clear liquid and then looks at Doreen. "As soon as I see him pull up, it's gone."

When she doesn't object, Phil slaps the table and unscrews the jar. The odor hits my nose like fire.

"Well, this should get interesting," Wayne says as Phil starts pouring the homemade liquor into the coffee cups. Everybody takes one. Sinclair swallows his in one shot, his eyes watering as he puts the cup down. When I reach for mine, Jake stops me.

"You've got to ship in the morning," he says. It gets a couple of groans from the table, Phil telling Jake to "let the boy drink, and that's what's wrong with the army, not a set among them." I pick up the cup, matching Sinclair's move and downing the liquid in one quick gulp.

It feels like I've swallowed fire, a sword, some kind of carnival trick, and I'm hacking, unable to talk as everybody at the table laughs.

"This boy's greener than a new dollar bill!" Phil says.

"I thought I was standing up straight, Sergeant," Ray says, slurring his words and making them all laugh harder. Even Jake smiles. "Exxscccuse meee."

"This boy needs another swallow for sure," Phil says, pouring me an even bigger helping, which I ignore. Pretty soon the conversation at the table is shooting back and forth, person to person, in one cloud of noise.

Phil seems to be laughing the whole time, pointing and talking animatedly about whatever subject comes up. But more than anything, I can't take my eyes off Jake. He hasn't taken a sip from his drink, but the anxiety and tension are slipping off his body like a pair of oversize pants.

"And then—God Almighty as my witness —he comes in and says, 'Cap-Captain, I swear it was there when we started!' "

As Ray finishes telling the story, the entire table falls apart with laughter. The whole of the Waffle House is watching, but who's going to say anything to these guys? To us?

Sinclair starts to tell us a story, but then Jake speaks up, as if he can't hear anything else that's happening. "One time we were out on patrol, foot patrol. And it's hot. Like over a hundred at nine in the morning."

The rest of the table grows quiet as Jake continues. It's the most alive I've seen him in months. He's rising up from his chair, moving his arms. He almost looks happy.

"So we're all sweating our asses off. Just dying. There's bugs everywhere, and there's this dude, a reporter—I don't even know who he was with—but anyway, he'd just shown up a week before." Jake starts ducking, twisting his face into funny mock expressions of terror. "You know what I'm talking about."

Ray and Phil both laugh, slap the table. "The worst," Ray says.

As he says it, Jake puts his head down, and for a second I'm worried he's going to fade out. That he'll ruin this, too. But when he looks up, he's laughing. "So anyway, we come up on this pool in the back of an old hotel. And it's perfect. The water all clear and bright. In the middle of this shithole, this pool."

"He didn't," Phil says.

Jake nods enthusiastically. "My buddy Donnelson is whispering in his ear the whole time. Telling him how good that pool would feel. How it's not against regs for him. Especially now. All the fighting was done, we thought."

Phil downs his 'shine, motioning for Jake to continue as he pours another shot.

"Next thing you know, the reporter is stripping off his suit, dropping everything in the dirt," Jake says, laughing. "And he just goes running. Sprinting toward that pool. I'm still surprised he didn't yell out, 'Cannonball!' Everybody on the team was yelling like crazy."

Ray and Phil are both shaking their heads, and Jake is laughing even harder, all of them tied to something I can't know. On its face I understand the story. I understand why it's funny and ridiculous that this reporter would drop all his gear and get in a pool during the middle of a war. I get that. But there's something behind the laughter, something that none of them can, or probably would, explain to an outsider.

For a second I want it again. I want this brotherhood, this ability to look another man in the eye and know that you have a shared experience. A connection that no matter what else you do in the world, how many times you fail or fuck up, you'll be able to measure yourself against. Something you've given your entire life for. A purpose. A meaning that's greater than nearly everything else in your life.

"I swear to God," Phil says. "If that happened in my corps, I'd kill the dumbass."

"Let's just say it was the last time the reporter went on patrol," Jake says. They all laugh, and Phil pours another round of shots. Wayne downs his; so does Sinclair. I lift mine to my lips but don't drink. I'm still reeling from the first ill-advised drink.

"You're the kid from the paper," Ray says, stopping every conversation in the restaurant. Or at least it feels that way to me. My chest tightens, and I'm afraid to move. To speak. I almost down the liquor until Jake nods.

"Yep."

"This is that kid they're naming the bridge after," Ray tells Phil. "Remember?"

"Holy hell," Phil says, standing up and saluting. There isn't a more earnest or genuine gesture I've ever seen. When he sits back down, he says, "They don't name a goddamn bridge after just anyone. Hell, no."

I search Phil's face for a hint of sarcasm, but there isn't a trace of it. Even wobbling, Phil is like my dad in his sincerity when it comes to honor and respect. When it comes to having a bridge named after you. Maybe it's the liquor, but I laugh.

Phil glares at me, like I slapped the waitress. I apologize immediately. "I'm not used to this stuff," I say, pointing at his jar. He doesn't lift his stare, his dark brown eyes serious.

"It's fine," Jake says. "Like I said, he's shipping tomorrow morning."

Phil's still staring at me when Ray asks: "Marines or real military?"

"Boy, you're pushing buttons," Phil says, reaching over and pretending to put Ray in a headlock. "By the look of him, I'd say that's a soldier all day long."

I'm not sure how to take that—compliment or slight—so

I don't say anything, and they both laugh. "He's messing with you," Ray says. "So, Fort Jackson or Fort Benning?"

"Jackson, sir," I say. The *sir* to impress them. The lie, a jab to my ribs.

"Lord, this kid's so green he's growing roots," Phil says.

"He'll do all right," Ray says, winking.

The waitress brings a pot of coffee, then dumps and fills the mugs scattered across the table. Phil tries to object, but she holds up a hand and says, "I'm not hearing it. Drink the damn coffee, Phil."

"How come you don't have a boyfriend?" Phil asks the waitress.

"Because all the men I meet are drinking 'shine at the Waffle House," Doreen counters. Phil holds his hands out to us like: What can you do?

"I'll quit drinking, quit running around," he says. "No more fun, just for you."

Doreen laughs, head back. "Wonderful. Let's run away together right now. I'm sure you're going to take care of my three boys, too."

They share a smile as she fills up his cup. "I'm too old and tired anyway," Phil says. Then he points to Jake. "But what about the young buck here?"

Doreen gives Jake a once-over, then glances at me. "I forgot to add: boys fighting in the parking lot. Another immediate turnoff."

"Blowing off some steam, that's all." Phil downs his coffee, and she fills it up. Doreen laughs, this time more to herself. She looks at Jake one last time and says, "I've got work to do, but y'all have fun."

When she leaves the table, Phil watches—not creepy, but like a proud father—and then turns to Jake and me and says, "Well, she does have a point. You two fighting and carrying on in the parking lot is about as stupid as it gets."

My words are knee-jerk and familiar. "It's nothing. We were only messing around."

"Shit, boy. You think I'm stupid?" Phil turns to Ray. "He thinks we're stupid."

"I've seen messing around," Ray says, pointing at Jake. "That wasn't messing around when you grabbed that backpack. That punch was real."

I stare at Jake, who isn't reacting to any of this. I wait for him to respond, to give any kind of defense. But he just sits there, like always, letting me do all the answering. All the work.

"Just brother stuff," I say, touching my eye.

Phil considers me for a long time before he says, "Uh-huh."

We're standing in a half circle around the back of Wayne's truck in the parking lot, talking. Wayne and Sinclair aren't saying much; it's mostly Ray and Phil alternating jokes with advice for my first day in basic.

"In my day you had something to worry about," Phil says. "But now, hell. They about hold your hand and help you wipe your ass. And they wonder why people are trying to push us around."

I'm supposed to tell them I'm not scared, but I don't think they'd hear me. Phil's slam on the army has Jake and Ray on fire, calling him an old man and laughing at his threats. Jake looks comfortable. These men bring something out of him, a vitality I've wanted to believe was still inside him. I soak in the normalcy, if only for a minute.

"Damn, you look like the world's ending," Ray says to me. "You okay?"

"He's going to be fine," Jake says, without the smallest glance in my direction. "He's almost ready."

"You got, what? Two? Three hours? Ray looks at his

watch. "You probably need to get home and get some sleep, brother."

"What he needs to do is go get his damn truck," Sinclair says. Wayne hits him. "What? It's just sitting out there. A man doesn't leave his truck behind."

"What's that mean?" Phil asks. "Where's your truck?"

"Stuck in some Sherrills Ford trailer park," Sinclair says, before I can make up an answer. I don't want them to know the hows and the whys of our being there.

Phil turns to me, his eyes on me like spotlights, the way my dad looks at me when he wants an answer. But unlike my dad, whose eyes are always filled with accusations and limits, Phil's are gentle but wild. As if he knows something. Even when Sinclair tells the story, Phil only nods. When he gets to how they cut the tires, it's Ray who turns to me.

"They cut your tires? Why?"

I hesitate. "I don't know."

"And what did you guys do?" Phil asks, looking at Jake.

When Jake doesn't answer, every bit of life draining from him once again, I speak.

"He pulled a knife on us," I say. "We couldn't do anything."

They don't ask why we were there, but I can tell Phil

wants to know. He looks from me to Jake and then finally back to Ray, who nods.

"Let's get that truck back," Ray says to him. They slap hands and then the tailgate of Wayne's truck, making plans and building up steam, as Jake continues to fade away.

"We don't have any tires," I say.

"I can get you tires," Ray says dismissively.

"It's five in the morning," I say.

"His dad owns Ray's Tire downtown," Phil tells me. "Next to the Chinese buffet?"

And then it hits me: I know who Ray is. His picture is on every wall of that place, and when I was growing up, whenever Dad needed to get the tires rotated or replaced, he and Ray senior would talk and boast. I wanted my dad to talk me up the way Ray senior would. I'd stare at those pictures of Ray, young and serious, and just wish. The Ray in front of me rubbing his eyes is a ghost of the kid on that wall. But back then he looked like he could walk through a building.

"I mean, you'll have to pay for them eventually," Ray says, pulling a key out of his pocket. "But seeing as it's an emergency, I'm sure we can get you rolling."

Wayne steps forward, like he's afraid to ruin the good times. "They're not telling you the whole story. These guys are—" I shoot him a look, shake my head. He sighs. "They're not good dudes."

"Well, they sound like a bunch of fuckups to me," Phil says, turning to Ray. "Go get the truck. We're doing this."

Wayne turns to me. "I can get your truck tomorrow. They sleep half the day. I'll go around ten and get it. I'll bring it back to your house, and it will be there when you get back from basic. But man, you know we can't go there." He looks over at Jake, who's fiddling with the straps on his damn backpack.

"As I live and breathe," Phil says. "Is there a sack among you boys? This is what's wrong with your generation. You're off watching videos on the damn computer and not getting out there and kicking ass. Fuck that. We're going."

Wayne groans, but Sinclair, despite everything, actually looks excited. Phil turns to Jake and says, "What do you think? You ready to see how a marine handles his business?"

"I'm not going," Jake says, flat. Still playing with the backpack.

"What do you mean you're not going?" Phil asks.

"I've got something to do," he says, glancing at me.

"Something to—this is your brother, man! Hell if you're not going." When Jake shakes his head again, Phil says, "A bunch of damn pansies, as I live and breathe."

Jake's leaning against Wayne's truck like it's the only thing keeping him upright. I don't care if he comes, but I have no idea how to explain that to Phil and Ray. How to be indifferent to what should be an absolute. And I understand his not wanting to go back to Clem's, especially with Phil. The questions would come. Why were we in a sketchy trailer park? Who are these guys? But I need my truck, and right or wrong, I'm not going to let covering for him ruin this, too.

"We don't need him." As I say it, my phone buzzes in my pocket. I don't look at it, just at Jake. He won't meet my eyes.

"Hell, no, he's coming," Phil says. "We don't leave men behind. Or trucks. I swear, where did you boys grow up? New York City?"

"I've got something to do," Jake says again, and Phil looks ready to tear his head off. He takes a step toward Jake but stops and closes his eyes. When he opens them, he speaks slowly and calmly.

"If you're anything like me, there's nothing you wouldn't do for your brothers, right?" Jake nods, but not as quickly as I expect him to. "This is your *brother*, but soon he'll be one of your brothers, too. So peddle that bullshit somewhere else, boy."

Jake gives me a long look before finally nodding.

CHAPTER SEVENTEEN

Wayne follows Ray's truck the mile and a half to his dad's store. Sinclair is in the bed with Jake, both of them flanking opposite sides of the truck. Even if they were talking, we couldn't hear. Wind whips through the windows, my hair. Nobody says a word. Wayne sighs deeply every few minutes.

When we get to the tire shop, Ray pulls up to a locked chain-link fence and hops out to open the gate. As we drive through, Wayne says, "Why are we doing this?"

"You know why," I say.

"We got off light. You don't realize that, but it's the truth."

"So I let them keep my truck? Fuck that."

Wayne shakes his head as he stops the truck, just behind Ray. Phil is already out and staring at us as Jake and Sinclair jump out of the truck and start casually picking through the stacks of tires.

"They won't keep the truck. They're just talking shit."

"What am I supposed to do? I need my truck."

"You're leaving in like three hours, you said. You don't need it."

I've already told Mallory; but this seems more difficult, and I don't know why. The words stumble out of my mouth.

"I'm not going to the army."

Confusion covers Wayne's face. "What?"

"I'm not going anymore. And I need the truck so I can get out of here."

Wayne blows air through his lips and opens the door, chuckling. I stop him and say, "Really."

"C'mon now."

"You saw Jake," I say, nodding toward the group. When I do, Sinclair yells to hurry up. "I'm not letting that happen to me."

My phone buzzes in my pocket again, but I'm too

exhausted to look. To be reminded that Mom and Dad are waiting for me. I fall back into the seat, close my eyes, and say, "So it's got to be now."

Wayne doesn't say anything for a second. He spins his key chain around his finger, the soft *tink-tink-tink* the only sound in the truck. "Damn, son. That's serious shit. Will they, like, arrest you or something?"

I shake my head. "I don't think so. Well, I don't know. It's not good, but what else can I do?"

"Does your dad know?"

I laugh. "No."

"Jake?"

"Just you and Mallory," I say. Sinclair calls out to us again, followed by Phil: how we're being pansies or something. Wayne looks at them and sighs one last time.

"You owe me so bad," he says. "You know that right?"

"Trust me. I know."

Wayne hits the steering wheel once and pockets his keys. "Well, shit. Here we go, I guess."

We hop out of the truck, and everybody's standing in a circle. Ray asks what kind of truck I drive, and he tells us the tires we'll need. It doesn't take fifteen minutes to find four tires, each one more worn and bald than the last, but they're good enough to get me out of the state. We load them into the back of Ray's truck as Phil goes around to the side of the shop and returns with a jack, some tire irons, and a power wrench, which Sinclair snatches up like it's candy.

"Hell, yeah," he says, torqueing it once.

"We don't use that unless we have to," Phil says. "Otherwise, we're in and out, quick and silent. Any questions?"

Nobody says a word, and Phil claps his hands together once. "All right then. Let's do this."

We park fifty feet from the entrance of the trailer park and start walking, tools in our hands and the tires on our shoulders. Phil leads us down the driveway, stopping when a car tries to start in the distance. Then we move again: ragtag and hobbled.

I can barely keep up with them, and even Ray is moving faster than I am. When we get to the truck, my phone buzzes again, and Phil gives me a look that is impossible to misunderstand. I reach into my pocket and silence my phone as he whispers instructions.

"Jake, you and Ray take this side. I'll take Sinclair and

do the other. Wayne, watch the house." He points at my leg. "You stand there and try not to hurt yourself."

Sinclair snorts, and Phil gives him the same look. "Okay, one, two, *go*."

They try to remove the lug nuts, but every one of them is stuck. Sinclair puts all of his weight against the small tire iron and says, "Damn. What did you do to these things?"

Phil gives it a try; but nothing happens, and he comes up cussing. Ray tries another nut, grunts, and then quits. He stands up and stretches his back. "I didn't think we'd need any WD-40, but these things are rusted like nobody's business." He shakes his head at my inability to care for the truck. "Can we call for a tow?"

Wayne gives it a go with the tire iron; but it bests him, and he sits down, breathing hard. "Might as well put a spotlight on us while you're at it," he says, throwing the iron into the dirt.

"We could pull it out," Ray says. "Got any chains, Phil?"

He shakes his head, and Ray bites his bottom lip, thinking. Sinclair steps forward with the power drill. "I can get those tires off in less than a minute."

Ray laughs, and Phil says, "Son, don't let that hooch

get you thinking you're Superman."

"It's too loud, Sin," Wayne says.

"It won't take but a second to do each wheel," Sin says. "You know I can do it."

Ray shakes his head. "I think we should stick with the irons. A lot less noise, and if you drop a nut, we're never getting this truck out. At least not today."

Sinclair looks offended. "I've never dropped a nut in my damn life," he says, turning his cap backward, the NASCAR logo showing, and before any of us can stop him, he makes the drill sing. The first tire is off before any of us can stop him.

Phil looks at Ray, shocked. "Well, shit. C'mon then."

The three of them work like machinery as Jake and I watch, but Sinclair is the star, moving around the truck like a ballerina, pulling wheel after wheel off and putting new ones back on. The drill is loud, too loud, but they've almost got the last tire on before Jerry Lee comes out of the trailer cussing. When he sees us, he jumps off the porch and yells, "Clem!"

Clem comes to the door, catching up to Jerry Lee. Phil taps Ray on the shoulder, and they walk to meet them. To my surprise, Jake joins them.

"Look at this," Jerry Lee says, laughing and waving his knife for emphasis. "Soldier boy went and raided the goddamn nursing home."

"How'd you like it if I took that knife and stuck it straight up your ass, boy?" Phil says.

"Perfect," Wayne says as they all start yelling about who's going to stick what, where. Wayne tries to stop me, but I walk toward them. "We just came for the truck," I say.

"And I told you to stay away," Jerry Lee says, pointing the knife at me.

"Raise that knife again," Phil says, "and you're not going to like how this ends, boy."

"Call me boy again and let's see," Jerry Lee says.

Phil smiles. Jake speaks.

"We're taking the truck," he says. "There's no problem unless you make one."

Clem steps forward and says, "That's where you're wrong, Jake. The problem is all these people coming here. It's the fact that the truck was *ever* here in the first place. So why don't you go fuck yourself and let these fine people come along for the ride?"

Jake doesn't respond; he's staring at Clem like a dog at

the end of his chain. Ready to snap.

"We're leaving," I say, reaching out and tapping Jake on the arm.

When I turn to go for the truck, Clem takes a step toward me, only to be met by Phil, Ray, and Jake. He laughs to himself, shaking his head.

It happens quickly. Jerry Lee lunges forward, and Phil dances sideways. Before I know it, Jerry Lee is on the ground and Ray is struggling to restrain Clem. Phil twists Jerry Lee's arm behind his back, all of it over in a matter of seconds.

"Get in that truck and get out of here," Phil says to me.

"We're not leaving you," I say.

For the first time Wayne agrees with me. "Jerry Lee, why do you always have to start shit?"

"I'm going to beat your ass, you little—ah!" Phil jerks Jerry Lee's arm up toward his shoulder blade.

"Don't you worry about these cheesedicks," Phil says, making Jerry Lee scream again. "And those tires are on me, okay? I'll settle the finances with Ray tomorrow. You and your friends get out of here."

I don't move. A quick look at Phil, and you'd think nothing was different from earlier this evening. He's smiling. His face is soft, almost relaxed. But there's something behind his eyes—a wildness—that I've seen too many times with Jake. It's how he looked right before he punched me. How he looks whenever somebody spends too much time asking him about the war, about how he's doing.

Before I can say anything, Clem breaks away from Ray and rushes Phil, knocking him over. As he goes down, Jerry Lee's arm snaps. He's screaming as Clem falls on top of Phil, punching him twice. Ray tries to get to Phil, but Jake is there in a flash. He pulls Clem off and holds him in the dirt, his forearm on Clem's throat.

Wayne and Sinclair pull Phil off the ground. Once up, he pushes them away and tries to go for Clem before Wayne grabs him.

"Take him back to the truck," Jake says, picking Jerry Lee's knife off the ground. "I'll take care of this."

Nobody moves, but alarms are going off all over my body.

"Big mistake," Clem says, and Jake pushes his forearm harder against his throat, choking away whatever else he's trying to say.

Jake looks at me and says, "You, too. Get your truck out of here."

"Jake, no."

"Get in your truck, Thomas."

The weird thing is, Jake looks more present right now than he has in months. Like he is in complete control of the fury that's gripping his body. I've never been more scared of him.

"Just leave it," I say. "Please."

"You don't understand," he says, pushing harder against Clem's throat as he holds his knife in his other hand. I say his name again, but he's leaning close to Clem's face, spitting as he talks. "You don't stand for shit. You know that? You don't stand for *shit*."

"Whatever you say, tweaker," Clem manages to say. "Good luck getting through the day after this."

I imagine Jake in the bright county jail suit, standing before a judge. The newspaper articles painting him as the villain. A trial. Having to visit him at Central Prison. Everybody will say they didn't see it coming.

"Bennett," Phil says, "you don't want to do this."

"He's a piece of shit."

Phil laughs. "Well, that's true. But taking care of a piece of shit ain't the mission. We got the truck, and these little pissants know exactly what will happen if they come looking for more."

Jake doesn't move, and Phil reaches out and touches him on the shoulder, just barely. "It's done."

Jake nods first, then slowly lifts his arm from Clem's throat. When he stands up, Clem doesn't move. Phil steps over him and says, "I swear, God as my witness, if you come near any of these boys, I'll break your goddamn neck. You understand me?"

Clem rubs his throat but doesn't say anything at first. Jake still hasn't dropped the knife. Phil carefully takes it and puts into his waistband, turning his attention away from Clem, who crab walks backward a good ten feet before he says anything.

"I'll kill you fuckers," Clem says, but it's toothless. It bounces off Phil and Jake like a toy dart. And right then I finally get to see Jake the same way as everybody else. The way I always had before. The kind of guy who'd walk toward hell because that's what's right, that's what's expected.

He looks like a hero.

As we head to my truck, I expect Clem to stand up and chase us down. To do something. But all he does is lie in the dirt and yell.

CHAPTER EIGHTEEN

The sun is coming up, a thin line of light drawn across the mountains as we drive back to the Waffle House. When we get back, everybody gets out, and I ask Phil if he's okay. He stands there for a moment, holding his ribs.

"Shit," he says. "Takes more than a bunch of damn titty babies to do me in."

Phil's words are like dawn bringing light, and everybody laughs, one big exhale. Even Jake smiles. Then Phil says, "That kid ain't gonna be pitching for the Braves anytime soon, is he?"

Wayne nods, but I can tell he's still worried. When Phil sees it, he comes over and wraps an arm around his shoulder. "Your brother ain't made of the same stuff you are, you hear me? Not even close."

Wayne nods as Phil looks over at Sinclair and says, "What about this kid? Like he was in the pits at Daytona!"

Ray pushes Sinclair playfully until his hat falls on the asphalt. As he picks it up, Sinclair says, "Hell, I probably could've done it ten seconds faster."

They laugh even harder, giving Sinclair shit. "Boy, you don't know a damn thing about nothing." But then Phil comes and pulls me aside. Jake looks over but quickly gets pulled into whatever story Ray is telling. Phil puts both hands on my shoulders and stares at me for a second, smiling.

"You ready for today?"

"Yes, sir," I say.

"Okay, okay." He looks over my shoulder, at the group of friends. "You know why your brother was with those guys, right?"

I hesitate. I've trained myself to not say anything to anyone. The last few months have been about smiling and agreeing and never—*never*—letting people on the outside know what was really going on. But Phil looks as if I could tell him anything. I don't know how to do it or if I even can. So I drop my head and don't say anything.

"I didn't know. Not until tonight."

"Hey, listen—listen to me." He bends over so he can look me in the eye. "You don't worry about your brother. We take care of our own. You understand that? When you leave, we got this. You understand me?"

The tears well up, a rogue wave of happiness. Or maybe it's simple relief. Whatever it is, all I can do is stand there with my arms hanging uselessly. He claps me on the shoulder once.

"Your brother's a tough son of a bitch," he says. "You may not be able to see it, but he's going to be okay."

I want to believe him. But Jake stopped fighting so long ago, and it feels like I did, too. "Sometimes I think he's not going to get better."

"He may need his ass kicked a little bit," Phil says, smiling. I must look confused because he says, "I'm saying we're going to watch out for him. That's all. Make sure he doesn't go off fucking around with any of the other cheesedicks out there."

"I think he needs help," I say.

Phil nods slowly, exhaling deeply. "Well, that, too. But son, nobody can do anything alone. And that's my point:

he isn't on an island. He's a part of me, and I'm a part of him; that's what it means to be brothers."

Phil stares at me as he finishes, his face certain. As if there weren't any other option. And maybe there isn't. Maybe that's the real secret of being a brother, the commitment that isn't based in obligation but in something deeper. Love? Compassion? And if Phil knew my plans, if he would try to talk me out of it right now, I just might go, restarting that old fire with words like *brotherhood* and *honor*. Everything I've seen on display in the past hour. That's all I ever wanted: people who would stand beside me no matter the odds.

"I'm scared," I admit.

He treats the statement with the same calm regard as everything else I've said.

"Anybody who says they're not scared is lying and most likely the biggest coward you've ever met. Everybody's scared, and you have good reason to be. Better than most. If you aren't scared, then you'll never be courageous."

The thought works its way inside me, expanding all the cracks of my plan with thick doubt. Could I do a complete 180 and by this afternoon be a full-on saluting soldier? I don't think so, but the way he's looking at me, the way he stares at me with his calm confidence, I still remember why I wanted to be.

"I'm going to go have a word with your brother," he says. "But then I want you two to get out of here, all right?"

He walks over and says something to Jake, the two of them separating from the rest of the group. As it happens, Wayne walks over to me smiling. I hobble and meet him halfway, at my truck.

"All right, Bennett." He reaches out and, yawning, slaps my hand. "For real, if you get into some shit and need a wingman, you call me."

Sinclair walks up as he says it, looking confused. "What are you talking about?"

"Nothing, man," Wayne says. "I'll tell you later."

Before they walk away, Wayne says, "Screw it," and pulls me into a hug. He nearly crushes me, but I put my arms around him. When we let go of each other, he fakes a punch at my stomach and says, "You're getting weak, son. Shit's pitiful."

As I watch them walk away, I'm struck by how much I'm going to miss Hickory no matter where I end up, a thought that until now hasn't really materialized for me. This town, these people are like DNA. Pulsing in my veins, making my body work. It's why I'm so worried about leaving, about letting them down. It's like denying a part of my flesh.

Phil is still with Jake. He points; Jake nods. He raises his arms animatedly, and Jake nods more. Ray has gone into the Waffle House, for a drink or to use the bathroom, and once Wayne and Sinclair roar off into the night it's just me leaning against my truck. The only sound is the cars on the highway and Phil, muffled but adamant.

I look around, more out of habit than any other reason. When I do, I see the backpack casually leaning against my front tire. I almost turn away before I realize what it is. But then it's all I can see. In the past few months I've never seen it anywhere but on Jake's shoulder, between his feet; it might as well be another limb. But here it is.

I act casual, trying not to draw attention to myself as I walk toward the front of the truck. When I get there, my hands are sweating. I could reach out and grab the backpack right now. Could run off into the night with it. Instead, I lean against the truck again, watching as Jake nods and Phil talks. They haven't looked at me once.

I turn around and unzip the black canvas bag with a near-perverted joy. It feels illicit the way my heart is racing.

When it's open, I don't know what I expect. Cash. Drugs. Maybe pornography. Instead, it's a rock. An unspectacular piece of sandstone about the size of a football.

"What the hell?" Jake says from behind me.

I spin around, the rock in my hands. When he sees it, his eyes go wide, and he takes a step back. "Put it back in the bag," he says quickly.

"What the fuck, Jake? This is what you're carrying around? A goddamn rock?"

"Put it in the bag," he says again. "Please."

I've never seen him this freaked out. He won't stand still; his eyes are like hummingbirds flitting through the air. I half expect him to swipe the rock from my hands and hold it close, like a child who's gone missing. Instead, he exhales and drops his head.

"Can we go somewhere else and talk about this?"

"Not until you tell me what this is about," I say, holding up the rock again. He won't look at it. Every time I move it, he cowers like a shamed dog.

Jake finally snatches the rock from me in one pained swipe. Once he's got it zipped back up and stowed behind the seat of the truck, he turns to me and sticks his hand out for the keys.

"We have to do this now."

"Do what?" I ask.

But Jake only shakes his head.

We drive slowly through the early morning, the birds coming to life all around us. The fatigue of the night is finally catching up to me, and the entire world feels fuzzy, drawn by a child. I have to pinch my leg to keep myself awake. Fifteen minutes of driving and we're parked in the turnoff area right before the River Road bridge. We sit there for a second, not saying anything as cars zoom by us—first shift at the mills.

"So . . ." I say, but Jake doesn't take the hint. He sits there, staring, thinking. About what, I can't tell until he nods once and says, "So we were over there. And it's just crazy, right? The entire town was already destroyed." He drops imaginary shells with his hands, blowing them up in his lap. "And there's this church, or maybe it's a temple. Either way, it's old. Like older than anything in this country by a thousand years, if not more. And it's all blown to hell. Just rubble. Guys were always grabbing stuff to bring home, you know? But I wanted something special."

He looks at me cautiously, as if waiting for me to catch up.

"So the rock is from . . . a church? Why does that matter?"

"We shouldn't have even been over there. That's the damn point." He hits the steering wheel and falls back into the driver's seat. He sits there breathing hard, not saying anything as I watch him.

"Dad won't like that attitude," I joke, but only for a second. His eyes are so serious, so vacant I'm not sure how else to respond.

"It's not a political thing," he says simply. "You know where I was?"

"The Middle East?"

He shakes his head. "The *cradle of civilization*. That's where the Garden of Eden was. That's where the devil came into the world, man."

We never went to church, not like a lot of people in this town. Maybe on Christmas or when my mom's extra-fundamentalist relatives would show up for a weekend. They'd drag us, wearing the only ties in the house, to whatever church they felt was *anointed,* and we'd sit through the sermon, through the healing, and then usually through a second, even longer testimony. But Jake has never talked about God once in his life, at least as I can remember it.

And here he is carrying on about Eden and the devil, and I'm not sure what any of it means.

"So, the devil—" I say. He pulls the backpack out from behind the seat and goes to open the door. I stop him.

"Jake, c'mon, man. What are we doing here?"

He shakes the bag and says, "We have to get rid of this."

"And what's that going to do? I don't understand what you're talking about."

Jake's eyes flash, and for a moment I think he might hit me again. I scoot back in my seat, but that's not it. When he pulls the rock out of the bag, he looks almost sick. He sits it on his lap, and we both stare at it.

"I fucked up when I took this," he says. "That's when everything went to complete and utter shit. Two weeks later the entire squad got attacked. The war was already over, man. And we get attacked?" He shakes his head, like he just walked into a cobweb. "I can't even get myself dressed in the goddamn morning, Thomas. I wake up, and everything feels too hard. Too much to even try."

I sit there, not sure what I'm supposed to say. How I can help him at this point? It's a rock, nothing more. But no matter how many times I tell him that, I don't think it will matter.

"You saved people's lives," I say.

He shakes his head, rubs his eyes. Before I can say anything else, he looks over at me and says, "I can't take a chance keeping this—especially if you end up over there, too. We need to balance the scorecard. We need to make things right because . . ."

He fades away, spinning. Gone. Normally when this happens, I walk away. But not only do I want him to finish the sentence, I'm not going. And if I tell him, maybe that will be the answer. Maybe that's been the answer all along.

He looks at me, eyes glassy. "If you went over there and got fucked up because I did something stupid, I'd never forgive myself. I need to fix this. You're my brother, man."

He looks up at me, like sharing this with me would somehow cause me to break away from him. I don't think twice.

"I'm not going to the army. I'm leaving."

He doesn't immediately respond, and I don't know how to say it any clearer, so I just shrug. When I do, he cuffs me in the back of the head and pushes me hard against the passenger side door. "What the fuck do you mean you're not going?"

"Look at you," I say. "How can I go? How do you expect me to go over there when you're—"

I don't think I can say it. But then he yells again: "Say it."

"You're all fucked up," I finally say. "And I don't want to come back like that. I don't think I can do it. If going over there did this to you, I'll never be able to handle it."

Jake sits back, the anger fading momentarily. He looks at the backpack in his lap and then, without warning, punches the steering wheel. I'm pretty sure he's broken his hand when he brings it back, but he doesn't react. Only stares at me.

"You committed," he says. "They'll throw you in the brig, Thomas. That's fucking *prison*."

I balk. I didn't know that would happen. If anything, I thought I'd have to mea culpa up over at the recruiter's office. Live with the shame. But *jail*?

The truck gets really hot, and I feel like I can't breathe.

"I'm going to—"

Jake cuts me off. "What? Do you really think Dad would let you do this? And even if he did, where are you going to go?" The disdain in his voice is worse than anything he could do to me. The way he's looking at me, like

I'm something that needs to be scraped off a boot.

"I don't know. California. Or maybe Canada. Somewhere."

"Are you fucking serious? *Canada.* Let's say that happens, what the hell are you going to do once you get to Canada?"

"I don't know," I say. "Work."

"Where were you going to live? How were you going to buy food? Do you have a passport?"

I nod halfheartedly, but I can't answer his questions. Even the answers I do have now seem unreasonable, a kid dressing up in his dad's suits and pretending to have a job. I look past him, to the road. It's 7:00 A.M., and I still don't have a clue about anything.

"If you do this," he says, "you'll never be able to come back. He'll never understand this, and you know it. And if you think he'll just let you go . . . well, you're a bigger idiot than I thought."

"I'll just leave. How will they find me?" I say.

"Yeah, I'm sure the United States government will have a really hard time finding you," Jake says, but his tone has softened. He leans back into his seat and cups the backpack on his lap. "Why didn't you tell me?"

I have no idea if I would've told him before he came back, when he was regular Jake, my brother. Would I even be in this position? I'd probably be at home right now dressed and anxious. Waiting for Dad to finish his coffee. Ready to roll.

But with Jake? I didn't think he would even be able to understand what I was saying, let alone give me advice. But I can't say that.

"I don't know."

"Bullshit," he says. "Don't sugarcoat it."

"I was scared . . . of you."

Before, he would've laughed, something. Now he only nods. I don't know what to say, how to proceed from here. Jake opens the door and gets out of the truck. When I don't follow him, he sticks his head in the window and says, "Get out."

We walk across the bridge, which looks subtly different in the light of day. Jake walks confidently, and I struggle to keep up, to fight the pain that runs through my entire body every time my foot hits the ground. When we get closer to where we stood last night, I almost expect to see one of Jake's medals on the ground, glinting like a diamond. Part of me wishes that's how the night would end, me holding up his medal. That it would somehow fix everything. But the only things I see are cigarette butts and bottle caps.

Jake sets the backpack on the side of the bridge, ignoring it when a passing car honks its horn. We stand there for a good minute before he says anything.

"If I don't take this rock, I don't come back a freak," he says. "If I don't take this rock, we're not even having this conversation. And in two hours you're on the bus and headed to boot, the way it's supposed to be."

I force myself to say something. "Jake . . . That's—"

Crazy. That's what I want to say. But I revise mid sentence. "The rock doesn't mean anything. All of this, what happened to you: the rock didn't do any of that."

He shakes his head, adamantly. "You don't understand because you haven't been there, Thomas. There are some things you just don't mess with. Things in the world that shouldn't be disturbed. I did this. And now I need to take care of it."

He doesn't move. He stares at the bag, a tortured look on his face. Every time he reaches for the bag, he stops himself and shakes his head, like he can't stand to touch the rock.

I don't think the rock is magical or evil. I don't think the devil is plaguing Jake or me. He's sick, that's it. But somewhere inside him, it is killing him. So real or not, it doesn't matter. I need to do something, finally.

I grab the backpack before he can stop me and throw it over the bridge.

It falls, falls, falls, finally hitting the water with a satisfying splash.

We stare down together, and at first I think Jake's going to reprise my dive into the dirty river. But he stands there, staring at the slowly disappearing ripples in the water until there's no sign of the rock, no sign that it ever existed.

"Do you think that will work?" I ask.

Jake stares down hard, not saying a word. I didn't think it would snap him back to life immediately, like something from a fairy tale. A weird kiss from the prince. But I did think he would react. Instead, he stares at the water until a car comes flying by, only looking up when the rear end of the El Camino has disappeared around the corner. My phone buzzes, but I ignore it. Almost immediately afterward, Jake's goes off, too. He looks at his and says, "Mom."

He answers it, and I already know the conversation

that's happening on the other end. "Where are you? Your father isn't happy. Come home." Jake answers all her questions, finally saying, "Yes . . . He's right here . . . Okay . . . Yes."

When he hangs up, he stares at me. "Dad is waiting for you."

A familiar stab of anxiety plunges deep into my chest. I want to run, but I can't. I want to drive away, but again: not happening. So all I can do is stand there, and barely that, feeling completely helpless.

"You have to stand up to this. You need to do what's right."

"I don't know what's right," I say.

"That's bullshit, and you know it."

"So I go home and tell Dad," I say, trying not to cry in front of Jake. When I look at him, it takes everything I have to keep myself together. "And then what?"

Jake stares at the water. "You want me to be honest?"

I already know what he's going to say. I'm sick because of it. I've known the answer my entire life. But I still nod.

"You go, man. You go."

"That's easy for you to say," I tell him. "There isn't anything you could do to disappoint him."

Jake gawks at me. "You're kidding."

"Do you realize what it's like having to live up to . . . you?" I say. "All I ever hear is: 'Look at Jake. Jake would never do it that way. Be just like Jake.' But I can't, okay? I can't be like you—not before, not now."

I'm breathing hard, barely able to get the words out. Jake shakes his head.

"Yeah, because my relationship with him is so great," he says. "He thinks I'm weak."

"Okay." I wave my hand at him.

"I heard him telling Mom one night. Because I came back like this. Because I can't just grin and bear it like everybody else. 'Soldiers before didn't come back broken.'"

I stand there, trying not to let his words—his logic—penetrate my plan, shaky as it may be. Every part of my body tells me to run, to escape, but is that just learned behavior? Or is Jake right? Will I ever be able to feel peace living this way? I turn around and lean against the railing of the bridge, closing my eyes. The sun is warm on my face as I speak.

"I don't know what to do."

Jake flicks me on the chest, and when I open my eyes, I'm not sure what's real and what's not. He looks no different from an hour before, but standing there with the sun outlining him, he looks bigger than life.

He waits for me to look him in the eyes before he says, "Yeah, you do."

My phone buzzes, and I nearly throw up. But when I look at it, it isn't Dad or Mom. There are five missed texts, all from the last two hours.

5:05 A.M.—*Hey.*

5:38 A.M.—*Listen, can we talk?*

5:45 A.M.—*Are you ignoring me?*

6:05 A.M.—*Hello…???*

6:55 A.M.—*I'm at the bridge. Meet me here.*

Mallory.

CHAPTER NINETEEN

As we drive, I try to figure out what to text back to her. If I go back to the bridge, what happens? What else is there to say? I'm sorry? Good-bye? Thank you? But what happens after that? How does anything either of us says change anything that's happened tonight?

Dad is waiting for us in the driveway, and when we pull up, he grabs me by the arm and drags me toward the front door. I'm howling with pain, and he doesn't notice until I'm two or three feet down the driveway. He bends and looks at my leg, then up at me.

"What in the hell did you do to yourself?" he says. "They're gonna send you to MRP, if they let you ship at all. Jesus Christ, Thomas, how could you let this happen?"

I don't say a word, and he stands up, his hands out to his side. "Am I talking to myself? Goddamn it, boy, I asked you a question."

"I don't know," I say. "I guess I just messed up."

"Messed up?" He laughs, but it isn't like any laugh I've ever heard before. "You didn't accidentally color on the walls. You've got sixteen stitches in that leg, at least. How am I going to explain this to Sergeant Veen?"

Jake is out of the truck, but he hasn't jumped in to explain anything. Mom stands close to him, checking his body as if she were going to suddenly find an injury twice as bad as mine. Dad hasn't looked at him once. But when he finally does, his eyes go red, and his volume comes up to a roar.

"How did you let this happen?" he asks. "This is your brother. You're supposed to keep him safe."

Jake doesn't answer, but he doesn't look away either. He stands straight, tall, barely blinking as Dad lights into him.

"What were you doing while he was off ruining his future? Answer me!"

"I was throwing my medals into the river," Jake says.

"And Thomas jumped in and tried to save them."

I've never seen Dad so flustered, so unable to mask how he's feeling. His face goes from shock to disbelief to anger like cards being turned over on a table. One after the other, just like that. When he still hasn't said anything, Jake turns to walk into the house, and Dad jumps across the driveway to stop him.

"Where do you think you're going?" he says.

They look like professional wrestlers as Dad tries to stop him from moving, grappling for dominance in the middle of our driveway. Every time Dad pushes, Jake counters. It's not until Mom yells for them to stop that Jake backs down. When he does, Dad puts him on the ground with one hard shove.

Dad is shaking when he turns to me. "Get your stuff together. We're going to the recruiter. Now."

"Dad," I say, my voice, my entire body—trembling.

Dad is calm, like the moment before a tornado is about to touch down. "Thomas, get your stuff and get in the truck."

"Can I talk to you?"

I don't know what to say, but I'm tired of lying. I'm tired of pretending that Jake isn't messed up, that I'm not scared. I'm so tired of playing a part that's been created for me. Whether I go or not, that feels secondary as I stand here. All I want is for him to listen to me, just once. To understand what it's been like keeping all of this inside me.

"Don't you see what's happened to him?" I ask.

Dad shakes his head. "Sometimes a soldier has to give something back to his country. That's the job. That's what you sign up for. Haven't I taught you anything?"

"Is it the job for us all to ignore it? To pretend like it isn't happening right under our noses?"

"Son, what do you think this is about? Do you think I didn't come back from Iraq feeling like shit? Of course I did. But I got a job. I was a father. If you don't understand what I'm telling you, maybe it's better if you don't go."

I've heard this speech thousands of times. Suffer silently. Be a man. I'm so sick of it. My phone buzzes, and when I look at it, Dad grabs the phone from me. As soon as he sees it, he nearly implodes.

"Is this your problem? 'Are you coming or not?'" He mimics a stereotypical girl's voice, throwing a hand in the air with a flourish. "You're willing to throw everything away for some girl?"

"It has nothing to do with her," I say.

Dad throws my phone at the driveway. It shatters, plastic and glass spray across our lawn. I stare at it, at him. And then I turn around and start limping back to my truck.

"Hell, no," he says, reaching for my shoulder. When he tries to spin me around, I slip away, even though my leg is killing me, and try to double-time it to the truck. He catches me easily and pushes me against the hood like a criminal. He stares at me without speaking, eye to eye like he's looking for an eyelash. A piece of glass. I don't look away. I try to channel everything Jake has ever been about, the fierce certainty he had with every decision.

He shakes his head, finally letting go of my shirt like it's covered in stains. Like he's going to get his hands dirty. Dad lets me off the hood and stares at me for a long time before he shakes his head and goes into the house. He doesn't slam the door, just closes it. The way he has a thousand other times in his life.

Mom runs over to me, but I don't know what to say to her. Everything I've wanted and planned for in the last few months is here, and I can't move.

"Honey, he doesn't mean it. He just wants you to be happy," Mom says. I'm too tired to argue with her, to clarify the definition of *happy*. Jake comes up beside her and stares at me, like he wants me to say something. Instead, I hobble past both of them and walk into the kitchen, where he sits, drinking coffee and staring at the newspaper. He doesn't say a word as I go to my room, as I reappear back in the kitchen with my duffel bag. I pause at the door, giving Mom a quick kiss. She tries to hold me back, to connect me to this place—this person—one last time, but I pull away.

Before I can get in the truck, Jake catches up to me. He closes the truck door and leans against it, crossing his arms.

"So?" he says.

"I'm still not going to the army."

"And what is that going to prove? That you're exactly what he thinks you are?"

"Maybe. But I can't stay here."

He nods and opens the door. "That may be true. But that doesn't mean you have to do something stupid to spite him." He motions for me to get in. When I'm in the driver's seat, the ignition cranked, he closes the door and leans into the window.

"Thomas, you might be scared, but you're not a coward," he says. "If you don't want to go, fine. Don't go. But you need to let them know. You need to stand up to it."

I only want to escape the responsibility. To drive away, pretending that he never went to war and that I never signed up. Play Lost Boy until the army or my father tracks me down. How many months could I grab before that happened? One? Five? But even as I think it, it feels wrong. A piece that doesn't quite fit in my puzzle. And as much as I want to deny it, I can't.

Jake reaches across me and works the stick shift into first gear. "Can you get it into second? You can drive it in second as long as the engine is running smooth."

"Do you really believe that?" I ask. Jake looks at the gearshift, still in first. "Not the truck. Do you think I'm not a coward?"

He looks surprised, almost offended, as he stands straight and looks from me back to the house. When he leans back into the truck, he stares into my eyes for a good ten seconds before he says anything.

"I think courage is somewhere between doing what you want to do and what you need to do," he says. "And that's on you, man."

He nods and clears his throat, pointing down to my leg. "Can you work the gas and brake?"

I test the pedal with my foot. Even though the pain forces my eyes closed, I nod. When I open them, Jake is still staring at me. I try to think of something to say to him, some kind of validation for the decision I've made. He smiles, slapping the roof of the truck once before turning around and walking back down the driveway.

CHAPTER TWENTY

I park at the top of the bridge, carefully lower myself out of the truck, and listen for Mallory's voice—for cussing or crying, I can't be sure. When I don't hear anything, all of the adrenaline disappears, and I crash. I slide down the embankment, not sure what I'll find, if she'll still be waiting. But like so many times before, when I duck underneath that crumbling concrete, there's Mallory.

"Shouldn't you be gone?" she says, monotone. Barely even looks at me.

As always, I have no idea what to say to her. I try to force a joke. "Aren't you supposed to be married by now?" But as soon as it leaves my mouth, I know it's wrong. It sounds petty, cruel. And I see her cringe.

"That was the plan," she says. I open my mouth, and she says, "Don't tell me you're sorry."

"I can leave."

"Well, go already," she says sharply.

"Hey, you texted me," I say.

We stand there, facing off like two kids, waiting for the other to speak, to move, to do anything.

"Yeah, like an hour ago. Glad you had time to fit me in."

I tamp down my indignation, the evidence I want to raise in my defense. I was getting the truck back. I don't have a phone. Jake. But she already looks defeated, her face smudged with dirt. As if she had been down here digging holes. I take a cautious step forward, slowly sit next to her.

She doesn't say anything.

"So, how was *your* graduation?" I ask. First she smiles; then she shakes her head. Like she doesn't want to let herself laugh.

"It's all unicorns and rainbows over here," she says. "You?"

"Pretty much the same."

She laughs once. "God, this is so fucked up."

I let that statement define the evening, everything about the last few months as we sit in silence. The new day streams before us, already getting warm. I can see cars in the distance, can hear a plane traveling overhead. I could sit here all day—for the rest of my life—and wouldn't be worse off.

"So, you're getting . . . married," I say.

She doesn't immediately react, just stares out past the bridge. A faint smile appears on her face. "What were we thinking? What a damn cliché."

"I don't know," I say. "He seems like a good guy."

"He is," she says, her words fading away into the growing sound of the cicadas. She turns to me and says, "I wanted to do it. I really did. But one day I started worrying: What if I meet somebody else later? What if we don't like living together? I don't want to end up like my mom, nineteen and pregnant. Working full-time to pay for day care."

"That sounds terrible," I say. She laughs, louder than I expect.

"I know. Why do you think I quit that shit?"

I laugh, too, and in that second it feels like I can breathe.

"Really." She continues. "It freaked me out. So last night at the party, I thought: Okay, just tell him you're not ready. He'll understand. But you know what happened."

"I could take you to see him," I say. She shakes her head, looking at me sideways.

"He's so pissed at me right now. After you guys left, we talked, and I tried to explain it. But all he could hear is you and me. I told him it wasn't like that."

She puts her hand on mine, and the weight of it is extraordinary. We're both looking out into the sun when she says, "You know I love you, right?"

My chest tightens because I've always known. Still, it's not the sort of thing we say to each other. We were beyond words, beyond needing anything to solidify who we were and what we meant. But now, with her hand on mine, how wrong could I have been? How easily you forget the essential parts of yourself.

So I say: "I guess I love you, too."

"Wow. Thanks for that, Thomas."

But she's smiling, still holding on to me like I'm a wayward balloon, ready to float away. And I just might. Hearing her say she loves me makes me sad because the only thing we have left to say is good-bye, to officially end this night. And that's not coming as easily. I don't want her to move her hand off mine either, because that's no different. A confirmation that the time has come and this is done.

I put my other hand on top of hers, and she one-ups me, like we're kids trying to figure out who gets to bat first. I smile. She laughs. Our hands separate, and the cool air on my palm feels awful.

She stands up and, facing me, pulls me to my feet. I squint into the hot sun as she buries her face into my chest. I don't want to be the first to let go, so I wait for her to do it, and a minute later she's wiping away tears and laughing.

"I don't know why I'm crying," she says.

"Because you're going to miss all of *this*." I flex, pose. She laughs.

"You're stupid," she says, hitting me once. "So . . . what happened?"

"I told them," I say.

"And?"

I shrug. She has to know how it went. "I'm going down to the recruiter in a minute. They're not going to let me go with my leg like this anyway, I don't think. But I need to go and at least talk to them. From there . . . I have no idea what's going to happen."

We stand there, facing each other, the skeletons of our childhood buried in the ground beneath us, the smell of the pine trees, the promises of everything we were to each other coming in every sound, every smell, every tiny speck of dirt that floats through the sunlight.

"Well, if you're still around," she says, "I think we should go back to the Grover tonight."

I laugh. "I have a feeling that I'm not going to be doing much of anything for a long, long time."

"Are you going to leave?"

I shake my head. And then we stand there, watching the sun rise higher and higher in the sky.

She moves first, leading me away from the bridge. As I struggle up the hill and she grabs my hand for balance, for leverage, I want to believe that we make our own plans. I want to believe that we are the ones in control of our lives.

But as Mallory Carlson gets in my truck—not for the last time because I know that can't be the truth—as we pull away from the bridge, as we make it onto the road and I drive toward her house, I have to believe in whatever magic brings us down twisted roads, leading us to places we never expected. Leading us back to the place we should've been all along.

ACKNOWLEDGMENTS

There are so many people to thank, and I have to start with my family. Michelle, Nora, and Ben allow me to disappear—both physically and mentally—in order to make these books happen. I appreciate that time, even if it's spent away from all of you.

Leon Guthrie (U.S. Marines) was integral in helping me wade through a culture I respect but know very little about. His knowledge of the military and his respect for veterans everywhere allowed me to really understand what it means to live a life of honor and courage—both before and after the military. He was the first person I ever met when I moved to North Carolina, and I'm happy to still call him a friend.

Ray Veen (U.S. Army) was also invaluable. As both a writer and a friend, he has never been too busy to listen or answer questions. I can honestly say I wouldn't be the writer I am today without his friendship.

I wish I could list all of the friends and mentors I've encountered in this world of book writing. Molly, Sara, Chris, Paul, Matt, Seth, Aaron, Kate, Steve, Jeff, and so many more . . . I am lucky to have access to such great people. Speaking of great people, I worked on this book while a student in the M.F.A. program at Seattle Pacific University. Thanks to Greg Wolfe and company for a truly life-changing experience.

Martha Mihalick edited this book and made it what it is. Her name should probably be on the cover somewhere— that's how much she does for me in this process. Thank you.

Michael Bourret, my literary agent, is always on board, no matter what I want to do. Well, maybe not the professional wrestling book. But . . . maybe? In all seriousness, there is no one better to have in your corner.